Love, Ocean

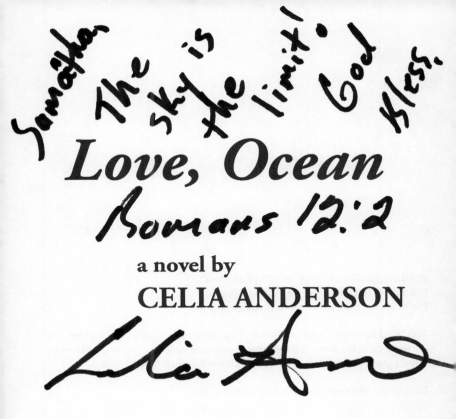

Samantha
The sky is the limit! God Bless.

Love, Ocean

Romans 12:2

a novel by
CELIA ANDERSON

Celia Anderson

Tempie Rene Publishing

Tempie Rene Publishing

Little Rock, Arkansas

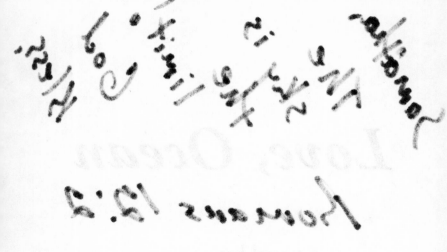

PUBLISHED BY TEMPIE RENE PUBLISHING
P.O. Box 4476 Little Rock, AR 72204-9998
For additional copies visit www.celiaanderson.com

Library of Congress Cataloging-in-Publication Data

ISBN-13: 978-0-615-22557-9
ISBN-10: 0-615-22557-9

Printed in the United States of America

First Edition

January 2009

10 9 8 7 6 5 4 3 2 1

For the citizens of New Orleans –
who refused to let their beloved city die.

Acknowledgements

I love my mother with every fiber of my being.

I know God is supposed to be first, but to me that's a given. So I have to open with my mother, Sarah Mae Hinton. Thank you for giving me all you have to give. I love you with my heart, soul and mind. To my baby girl, Gabrielle Simone Anderson, niece Tempress Sanaa Wimberly and nephew Emmanuel Jerard Wimberly, thank you for teaching me how to love. I promise to try my hardest never to let you all down. To my big sister Latonia Wimberly and my baby sister Shannon Lee Anderson, they can say what they want about our father; he may not have given us much, but he gave us each other and for that I am eternally grateful. Simmery Yvette Thompson, you are so much more than a friend; you too, are a sister.

Robert Austin Anderson, you are and always will be my only brother and I love you dude. To my father, Carl Kenneth Anderson, the last few days we spent together were the best days of my life. At first I didn't understand why you were taken from me so soon afterwards, but at least after 29 years of not knowing what a father's love felt like, I got to experience it, if only for a little while—rest in peace.

I have a lot of family, but very few rocks. My grandmother, Tempie Rene Wells, great aunts Avera Kirkwood and Fannie Mae Kirkwood, great uncle Larkin Kirkwood, I love you and thank you so much for your legacy of strong wills and kind hearts. Willie Albert Hinton and Melvin Kirkwood—talk about raising a child by committee! Uncle Will, thank you so much for loving me like I am your very own, and Uncle Melvin, you just don't know how much watching you has made me realize just how a man is supposed to treat a woman. David Saffold, Johnnie Bonner and T.W. Hinton, I can't leave you out of the uncle group. Thank you for the years of laughs and for always making me feel beautiful.

To my grandfather, John Henry Hinton, from day one, you were my guy. I love you and I miss you. My paternal grandmother, Ethel Lee Anderson, thanks for being my example of greatness. Aunt Annette Johnson, thank you for keeping it real and helping me through; your heart is pure gold—I'm sure of it. Uncle Ronald Anderson, you are and always will be my hero. Time will never take that away. Dorothy Anderson and Doretha Rose, thank you for showing me how to make something out of nothing. Without your example, I may have given up on life a long time ago.

Brace yourselves for this next list - I have a whole host

of cousins, and I have to mention each one specifically because they all hold a special place in my heart. Demetrius and Jasmine Carter, I love you. Dee, because we grew up together like brother and sister; no one can take our history from us. Jasmine, I know you love my cousin more than life itself. Shannon Boyd Jr., where do I begin? Cuz, I love you man. It was instant from the first time we met. Wish I lived in L.A. I know we would be inseparable! Shantell Renee Hinton, you are an awesome young woman, worthy of only the best. Never forget that. Derek Hinton, big dreams eventually become reality. Thanks for dreaming with me. Keira, Jameshia, Jamarrius, Devontarrius, Adrianna and Gary, keep the legacy alive, little cousins; we expect great things from you all, because we all know there is greatness in you.

Iris Saffold—I have to give you your own paragraph. How can I not? A young woman who has endured all you have deserves special attention. I love you, cousin. Not just because we are family, but because you are so amazing. You have your mother's spirit and your brother's charisma (R.I.P. Aunt Jackie and Lil David). How can you fail? I'm in your corner always.

Bobbie Kirkwood and Delona and Gary Moore, I could not ask for better big cousins to lean on when life threw its best blows at me. Thank you for opening your homes and for your words of wisdom. Debra and Laquita Kirkwood, though life has taken us different directions, I love you both and I will never forget our days in Greenwood, MS. Those times are engraved in my being. From 611 Henderson Street to Davis Elementary, I shall never forget. Tiffany, LaShawn, Melanie, Terrell, Tasha, Terrance, Terron, Terrious, LaRon, Dennis and Tray, the Anderson gene is so tough! How else would we have made it? Each time I see you, I see reflections of myself. I love you all.

Clarence Haynes, Tony Boyd and Patrick Oliver, thank you for being my guiding light throughout this entire process. Sharon G. Flake, thank you for paving the way—without you, there may have been no me. E. Lynn Harris, I learned lifelong lessons from being in your presence. Thanks for being my teacher.

Doris Gaiser, Claudia Rodgers and Linda Jones, your dedication to me early in my life is the reason I am who I am today. God got it exactly right when he made the three of you. To my former coaching staff at the University of Arkansas, Gary Blair, Vic Schaffer, Amber Shirey, Trenia Tillis and Kelly Bond, thank you for giving me a chance. I may not have understood the blessing then, but I am who I am because you chose me to be a Razorback. Melissa Harwood Rome, Chancellor John White and Bill Smith, thanks for not judging me and taking the time to get to know me. Tennille Adams, Nicole Bynum, Yolanda Amos, Khalil Carter, Vincent Dodson and Kela Peterson, thank you for being my very best friends during my college years. I never could have made it without you guys. Former teammates Daisha Reed, Rajiah Matthews, Amy Wright and Katrina Nesby, who would have thought then that I was making life long friends? Thank you all for putting up with me!

Acknowledgements

Very special shout-outs to Wanda Harris, Darchell Leggett, Kristie Baxtor, Cher Roberts and Nicci Howard. Thank you for believing in me and being the very best friends a woman could have during difficult times. My good friend, Addis Huyler, I love you; keep your head up. Quashanta Martin, Samuel Hall and Desmond McDaniel, you don't know how special the time that we all spend is to me—so nice to be able to come home to realness. True Essence of Delta, you know I wouldn't forget you ladies. What amazing women we have grown into! Kendra Taylor, thanks for being down from the start. I love my DST!

Dr. Gabriel Crenshaw, thanks for keeping me sane! Dr. Corey DeWayne Harris, thanks for being the steadying force in my life.

Last but certainly not least, I have to mention four very special men who, although they probably don't know, during my teenage years collectively fathered me. Sam Mundy, Charlie Johnson, Thomas Poole and Darrell Brown, Sr.—for a lost girl like I was, you really made the difference.

I hope I have made everyone proud. It really does take a village. Until next time...

-Celia

Love, Ocean

Chapter One

I know I love Jovan.

My daddy says that I'm too young to know what love is, but my heart says he's wrong.

"Did you study last night?" I asked. Jovan and I had just finished eating lunch and were waiting for the bell to ring.

He gulped down the last of his Gatorade, and then asked, "For what?"

"Our English test."

"Man, I forgot all about that test."

"It's all essay. Did you at least read the story?"

Before he could answer, there was an announcement over the intercom, "Ocean Sims, please report to the office for check out."

"Did they say my name?" I asked. No one said anything to me about being checked out of school today.

"Yep. They said you. Where you going?"

We stood up, "I don't know."

Jovan slipped his arms over my shoulders and I buried my face in his chest. After a second or so I turned to the side and rubbed my cheek against the long white tee he was wearing. We stood there for almost a minute before he leaned in and kissed my forehead. His lips were soft and gentle. I love the way his six four frame towers over me. I always feel safe when he's around. We have been together for three years. The first one was a little rough, because I had to deal with females flirting with him all the time. Before long, I realized that he never returned the favor and was completely devoted to me. Since then, we have grown closer than I ever thought possible.

He is my soul mate. I know it.

Finally we pulled away and I looked up at his perfectly sculpted face. The hairline that circles it is one of his most attractive features to me, especially when he is fresh out of the barber shop. The small diamond stud in his left ear is the only interruption in the flow of his dark skin. I touched his cheek.

"I will text you when I find out what's going on," I said.

"Okay."

"Love you."

"Love you too."

I put my purse around my shoulder, gave Jovan another quick kiss, and headed to the office for check out.

When I walked into the front office I was shocked to see Mrs. Pitman, my best friend's mom. She was wearing baby blue scrubs and a look of worry.

"What's going on?" I asked, wondering how she'd managed to get away from her job at the daycare. The government makes her volunteer there. It's the only way she can keep her assistance.

"Didn't Tisha text you?"

I reached in my purse for my phone. "I don't think so."

"Well your father asked me to put you and your grandmother on a bus to Houston."

"Houston?" I asked as I scrolled through my text messages. I hadn't gotten one from Tisha. "Why are we going to Houston?"

"This hurricane is getting pretty serious. Your father says he wants the both of you out of New Orleans."

Mrs. Pitman gave the secretary a small wave as we walked out of the school and climbed into her Ford Escort.

Hurricane Katrina had been the talk of school all week. We were watching the weather forecast in almost every class since the storm had become a tropical depression. But I thought my father was overreacting.

"What's in Houston?" I asked.

"Your Aunt Sheila is going to pick you up there, then drive you to Little Rock."

"Aunt Sheila," I proclaimed with a roll of my eyes. I hadn't spent a lot of time with Aunt Sheila, but none of the encounters had been good ones. They always started with her having too much to drink, and ended with a fight. Grandma says she don't know what's wrong with her. She raised her and my daddy the same, but Sheila turned out to be nothing but a headache.

I thought back to the last time I saw Aunt Sheila. It was Christmas about five years ago. She got so drunk my daddy put her out. He said she wasn't going to disrespect his mamma's house or me like that. Personally, she wasn't bothering me. I thought she was funny. Walking around like a toddler on skates. But daddy wasn't having it. Since then, we made an occasional drop-in visit to Arkansas, none of which lasted longer than a couple of hours.

"You hungry?" Ms. Pitman asked.

"I just ate," I replied.

I slouched into the passenger seat and folded my arms across my chest. I didn't understand what all the fuss was about. Weather predictions are wrong all the time. I had so many questions. What about Jovan? He hadn't said anything to me about leaving town. And why didn't my daddy talk to me about all of this? First of all, I don't like Aunt Sheila. And second, New Orleans is my home. How could someone make me leave my home and not even discuss it with me first?

The more I thought about it, the angrier I became. Finally I said, "I guess how I feel don't matter, huh?"

"Ocean," Ms. Pitman said in a stiff tone. Although she's not my mother, she treated me like I'm her daughter. "Let's not make this difficult," she continued. "This hurricane is serious. Everybody is trying to get out of here."

"Then why ain't you leaving?" I snapped back.

"Don't you think I'm trying? I have a daughter who needs to leave just as bad as you. We are trying to hold out until I get my check on the first," she said. "And fix your language. I'm sure you learn proper English in school."

I ignored her last statement. I know how to talk right when I need to. "What about Jovan?" I asked.

"I'm sure his parents will figure out something for him."

"He ain't got no parents."

Ms. Pitman cut her eyes at me. I couldn't tell if it was because of the double negative I had just used or my mention of Jovan. She doesn't like Jovan. Says I can do better. When she met him he was dressed in baggy pants with a Ben Franklin football tee. So she automatically assumed he was a dumb jock. The truth is she just happened to meet him on one of his off days. He is very diverse in his dress. It's nothing to catch him in khakis and a button down.

"Jovan is not my concern."

The tone of her response told me I should shut up. I had already pushed her far enough. I let out a sigh, then flipped open my cell phone. I had to text my man.

My dad's making me go to Arkansas, I wrote.
Y? He texted back a few minutes later.
He's scared of the hurricane.
How long?
IDK. Hopefully just the weekend.
Well, hit me when you get back.
K. Love U.
Love U2.

Love, Ocean

Well at least this little trip won't cost me my boyfriend, I thought.

Chapter Two

After sitting for almost two hours in the worst traffic I had ever seen in New Orleans, we finally made it to the Greyhound bus station. Tisha and my grandmother were there waiting for us. Inside the station was complete pandemonium. Workers visibly irritated and passengers even more so. One lady stormed out of the station in tears when she was told that there was no room on the bus for her and her six small children. One guy was carried off in handcuffs for trying to force his way in front of others who were waiting to board. The scene reminded me of the images I'd seen of Wall Street during the big time Hollywood movies. Everybody was talking loudly and in complete disarray.

"Thanks," Grandma said to Ms. Pitman as we approached them. "It was no way I could drive in all this mess."

"No problem," Ms. Pitman responded before turning

her attention to Tisha, "How long did you have to wait in line for the tickets?"

Tisha looked down at her watch, "We got here at nine a.m." It was three o'clock. "All of the buses are sold out."

I guess it was Tisha's job to drive my grandmother to the station and buy the tickets, and Ms. Pitman's job to get me from school. I started to ask for details, but figured they were not important.

"I'm glad you came early," Ms. Pitman said. I heard a tremble in her voice that exposed fear I think she was trying to hide. I looked up at my grandma. Then she and Ms. Pitman exchanged a terrifying stare. I had only seen that look once from my Grandma. It was the same one she gave my daddy the day he left for Iraq. Finally, after what seemed like an eternity, my grandma spoke.

"They will be okay," she said placing her hands on Ms. Pitman's shoulders.

They? What did she mean *they?* Before I could ask, Ms. Pitman spoke up.

"Mrs. Washington, I know I told you these tickets were for the girls, but your son bought these for you and Ocean. Now I will pack your stuff—"

"Well I don't know why in the world he did that. I ain't

9

going no where!"

"Mrs. Washington, please-"

"Please nothing. I should have known there was something going on—having this child pick me up early. Talking about she needed an adult to get the tickets. Anybody can buy Greyhound tickets."

I laughed at my Grandma. Ms. Pitman can give this one up. I didn't even know why daddy put her up to it. He knows Grandma loves this place. We couldn't even get her to go on vacations with us.

"This is going to be serious, Mrs. Washington," Ms. Pitman was pleading.

"I stayed through Betsy, and I'm staying through Katrina. Now if Willie wants his child to leave that's up to him, but I'm not his child!"

"Mrs. Washington, please?"

Ms. Pitman gave it one last try. For a second I thought maybe my grandmother would just get on the bus.

I was wrong.

"Now I done said all I'm gone say now," she threw her hands in the air like a choir director, "You can put them girls on that bus, but I ain't going no where!" She shook her head so hard her wig shifted a little to the right.

Ms. Pitman didn't reply. Instead tears welled up in her eyes then spilled over her bottom lids like ocean waves. Tisha wrapped her arms around her mother's tiny frame.

"Mamma, don't cry," she said. "She can leave later if things get bad."

For some reason, her mother seemed unmoved by Tisha's words.

"Why can't we all just wait and leave together?" I asked.

Ms. Pitman grabbed the bottom of my chin, "Leaving now is best. I can't make your grandmother leave, but you are getting out of here."

"What are we going to do with the other ticket?" I asked.

Ms. Pitman clasped her hands together and looked up, "There is a God," she said, then turned to Tisha.

"Go change the name on that ticket. You are going to Houston."

Chapter Three

I, Ocean Renee Sims, never thought I would find myself away from my daddy *and* grandma. But somehow it's happening. All my life I have been back and forth between the two of them. When daddy is busy with the army, and most of time he is, I am with grandma.

I was born on Ft. Knox army base in Kentucky. My daddy always jokes and says that he gave birth to me. He has been a single father since my mother left when I was two. Daddy says she just woke up one morning and said she couldn't do it anymore. I used to wonder about her when I was younger, but now at seventeen, I'm okay with it. Like the old cliché goes, can't miss what you never had.

"What's contraflow?" I asked the bus driver as he loaded my bags in the bottom of the bus.

"That means the expressway heading into the city is

closed, allowing outbound traffic to travel both sides."

Why didn't the announcement over the loud speaker just say that? I thought.

"Thanks."

"What'd he say?" Tisha asked from over my left shoulder.

"He said it meant the freeway is closed."

"Oh." She paused. "Well, how are we going to leave then?"

"My bad. I meant just the freeway coming into the city. That's why the announcement said there were no delays."

"Dang, they closed down the freeway? This storm is serious huh?"

"Your mamma said it is going to be bad."

"I know. She never really reacted like this before. I mean, I don't even have any luggage. Plus, she would never let me go to Houston by myself. How many times have we asked her to go visit Tasha?"

Tasha is Tisha's older sister. She goes to college in Houston. At least that's what she says. Every time she comes home grandma says, "That child ain't bit mo in college than the man on the moon! College girls wear way more clothes than that!" Maybe grandma is right. That's why Ms. Pitman would never let us visit Tasha no matter how many times we asked.

"It is kinda weird, huh?" I asked.

"What's weird?"

"You going to stay with Tasha." Sometimes I think Tisha has forgotten (or never learned) to use her brain.

"Oh, yeah," she giggled. "You know something must be up if momma is letting me go there."

"Well at least you don't have to go to Arkansas."

"Ain't that the truth? Maybe you can take some of New Orleans with you in a can," Tisha joked.

We shared a well-needed laugh.

After standing in line another ten minutes, we finally boarded the bus. It was crowded and smelled like my fathers workout clothes when he left them in the laundry room too long. I passed by several open seats before I found two next to each other for us. I slide past the elderly gentleman in the aisle seat and sat down next to the window.

"Man, why I got to sit in the middle?" Tisha said.

"Because you were afraid to get on the bus first," I teased.

Tisha is the pretty one. With her long coal black hair and wide eyes with long lashes to match, she drew the kind of attention that I sometimes wish I did.

I am the brave one. One Halloween we went to a haunted house, and she was so scared she peed herself. I laughed all the way home. She made me promise not to tell anyone. I didn't either, until freshman year when we had our biggest fight ever. She told a boy I liked that it didn't matter if I was pretty or not—I was a nice girl (another one of her brainless moments). She thought she was helping me. But it hurt my feelings for my best friend to basically call me ugly. Before I knew it, I yelled in front of the whole class, "I may not be as pretty as you, but at least I don't pee on myself." (She's lucky that's all I said. I wanted to say that at least I'm not as *dumb* as you).

Tisha got completely quiet. She and I didn't talk for two whole weeks. Then she got into it with some girls. I can't remember their names, but they hated Tisha. Anyway, I walked into the lunchroom, and one of them had her finger in Tisha's face and was rolling her neck like it was a slinky. In one instant, I threw my backpack to the floor, and ran to where they were. Luckily (for them), a teacher broke us all up. That put the seal on our friendship.

Now we are sisters.

"You burn that new Destiny's Child yet?" Tisha asked.

"Jovan bought it for me."

"I wish my man would buy me something. He acts like it has to be a holiday for me to get a gift. You got a good man."

I smiled inside then said, "I don't know how I am going to make it through the next couple of days without him. I can't wait until all of this is over. I would have held him longer in the lunch room, if I knew I was leaving."

"Well, I saw Charles last night."

"Last night?" I cut my eyes at her. "Where?"

"His dorm."

"Tisha," I said, remembering all the trouble she got herself into last summer with Charles. "What did you do?"

"Nothing. Just gave *him* a little something."

"How was it?"

"It hurt at first like always, but then it was okay."

"Did you use something?"

"We didn't have time for that."

Before I could tell her how dumb she was for not using protection, my cell phone rang. Although I could tell by the ring tone it was Jovan, when I looked at his face on my screen, I felt like someone had dipped my insides in warm water.

"We're not done talking about this," I said to Tisha,

then answered my phone.

"Hey," I said innocently.

"What's up boo? Where y'all at?"

I was blushing. I love it when he calls me boo. "On the bus."

"The bus? Yo pops is serious, huh?"

"You know how he is. Don't want anything to happen to me."

"You know I know. Tell grandma to hold it down."

"She didn't come."

"So you by yo'self?"

"Tisha with me."

"Tell her water head self I said hey."

"Jovan says hello," I said to Tisha.

She leaned close to the phone. "Hey Jovan," she said, "Keep an eye on Charles for me."

"You hear her?" I asked.

"Yeah, I heard her, but I can't help her. That's between them."

"He said okay," I replied.

"Why you lying?" Jovan exclaimed. "You know I didn't say that. I'm not in that."

"Where are you?" I asked, changing the subject.

"On my way to the crib. They cancelled our game and there's no practice."

"Good. That way I won't miss it." Jovan is a senior wide receiver for our football team. I have not missed a game in two years.

"Not good for me. You know my future coaches were coming to this game." Jovan also signed with Louisiana State University at the end of his junior year. He is one of the top players in the state.

"That's right. I forgot. They will get to see you play when all of this is done."

"I hope so man. You know their season starts soon. They won't have time to come to my games once that happens. Hold on a second baby okay?" his phoned beeped.

While I was on hold I thought about Jovan going to LSU. At least he wouldn't be too far from New Orleans. Plus, I was thinking of going to Fisk. I didn't want to leave Grandma.

"Ocean," Jovan came back.

"I'm here."

"Let me hit you back, okay? This is Coach Davie. He says we should think about going to the Superdome if we're not leaving town."

"Okay," I replied, then closed my phone.

I thought about continuing my conversation with Tisha since she did something stupid last night, but what Jovan said threw me off.

The Superdome—why would his coach tell him to go there?

Chapter Four

Dear Daddy,

I'm on the bus headed to Houston. As always, Ms. Pitman did just what you asked. Only she couldn't get Grandma to come. It wasn't Ms. Pitman's fault though. You know how Grandma is. Tisha ended up riding with me. Right now we are about an hour outside of Houston. I hope Aunt Sheila is there without her bottle. At first I was mad that you would send me to her, but once I thought about it, we don't have much family outside of New Orleans. I guess you didn't have another option (although I think this thing will blow over). I'm cool with it now though. I'll just make sure Ms. Pitman gets me home next weekend. I can deal with Aunt Sheila for a week I guess.

Anyway, don't worry about me. I'll be fine—will write you again soon.

Love,

Ocean

I folded the letter up and placed it in my backpack that was on the floor between my legs. My daddy makes me write him. I didn't understand it at first, especially since we also talk on instant messenger and he knows everything I put in the letters before they reach him. But he says writing is therapy and he wants me to feel like I can talk to him anytime. So if I log onto IM and he's not logged on or he doesn't get a chance to call, I can just write him. I didn't like writing at the beginning. Now, I love it. In fact, I write him more than I email. And nothing feels better than getting a reply from him in the mail. He always gives me good advice. The letters make me feel like he is only a pen stroke away.

"Where are we?" Tisha asked, stretching her hands overhead. We had both fallen asleep shortly after we left New Orleans.

"Almost to Houston."

Tisha rubbed the sleep from her eyes then reached overhead to turn on her light. "How long you been up?"

"About two hours."

"You couldn't sleep, huh?"

"Nah."

"Thinking about your dad?"

"And Jovan."

"I haven't heard from Charles," she said looking down at her phone. *Why would you*, I thought. *He got what he wanted.*

"I'm not surprised," I said before I thought about what those words would do to her feelings.

"Why you say that?"

I wasn't sure what I should say. I wanted to say, "Snap out of it. Charles don't want you. Can't you tell? All your thoughts are filled with him, but to him you're just an after-thought." Instead I said, "He isn't the telephone type."

"You're right," Tisha smiled. I think my words had given her yet another excuse for putting up with Charles and his games. I don't understand them. He's a sophomore in college and she's a junior in high school. Somehow he's convinced her that he loves her no matter what his actions are. She only sees him from time to time and his phone calls come as often as Christmas. Still, in her mind, they have a relationship.

I went into my backpack again; I have to ask my dad a question. While reaching for the letter, I noticed my music book. I thought I had put it in my locker. I'm glad to know I brought it; at least I could work on learning some new songs while I'm in Arkansas. I unfolded the letter and wrote:

Celia Anderson

P.S. Daddy, how do you know when someone loves you?

Chapter Five

"What if my mom is right?" Tisha asked as we said our goodbyes. We had arrived in Houston and both Tasha and Aunt Sheila were there waiting for us.

"She's not," I said bravely. I knew Tisha was afraid. "We'll be back home in no time."

"I hope so. I don't know what I'm going to do without you Ocean."

"Well we don't have to think about that. Text me later. We have a seven hour drive to Arkansas; I'll be looking for something to do."

"I will. Love you sis."

"Love you too Tish."

We gave each other one last hug and I headed towards the Cavalier that Aunt Sheila was driving. Judging from the green E on the bumper, it was a rental. Tasha was driving a

Benz.

Aunt Shelia took one of my bags and put it into the open trunk.

"How was the ride?" she asked.

"It was cool."

"Where's your grandma?"

I guess no one had told her either. "She didn't come."

"Didn't come? What you mean she didn't come? Willie said he was sending the both of you."

"He bought two tickets, but Grandma wouldn't get on the bus."

"Well, who supposed to look after you? I got a life and I ain't trying to give it up."

"I'm seventeen," I said.

"Don't think you grown," she snapped. I could already tell this was going to be a long visit. I hadn't been with her five minutes and she's already talking about how she doesn't have time for me. I decided that I would just keep my mouth shut and suffer through the next couple of days until I got back home.

"Can you call Willie?"

"No," I rolled my eyes as I turned my back to her. Why would she think I could call my dad? He was fighting in a war. What would they do? Go pull him off a tank and say, "Sergeant Sims, you have a phone call?" What an idiot. I opened the passenger door, plopped down in the seat and took my iPod from my backpack. I wasn't about to talk to her another minute. I scrolled through my list until I found Fantasia; then I pushed play, buckled my seat belt, and leaned safely against the door. I'm glad I didn't sleep much on the bus. Maybe I could sleep the whole drive to Little Rock.

Luckily, Aunt Sheila didn't bother me.

Chapter Six

I woke up in a cold sweat.

I dreamed my daddy had gotten shot. I'd been having this dream since he left; normally I wake up just as the bullet pierces his chest. But this time, I stayed asleep until his body hit the ground. It seemed so real. Opening my eyes to the Arkansas expressway, I was glad to know it was just a dream.

I glanced over at Aunt Sheila and for the first time during this trip really sized her up. She was dressed like a top model gone bad. Her jeans were at least two sizes too small and her breasts were squeezed so tightly inside a bright red corset that they were gasping for air. She was doing way too much. I didn't like her. I could see why my dad never really kept in touch. I removed my headphones from my ear and picked up my cell phone. No missed calls, but five new text messages.

Before I checked them, I called my grandma.

"Hello," she said after the fifth ring. It always takes her awhile to get to the telephone. It's in the living room and she refuses to get a cordless.

"Hey grandma," I was happy to hear her voice.

"Hey baby, where y'all at?"

"I'm in the car with Shelia."

Before either of us could say another word Shelia jumped in.

"Ask her why she didn't come? What? My house ain't good enough?"

"Did you hear Shelia, grandma?" I asked.

"Naw, baby what she say."

"She said why didn't you come?"

"Tell her I told her the last time I was there, I was never coming back. If it was up to me, you wouldn't even be there!"

I don't want to be in the middle of this so I handed Shelia the phone. As soon as she said hello, I could hear my grandma going off on the other end.

"Whatever mamma," Shelia said. "I don't know why I even expected you to come here." She threw the phone back in my lap. I picked it up.

"Hey grandma."

28

"You keep an eye on that crazy chile, and don't believe nothing she tells you, she is the biggest liar I know!"

"Yes ma'am."

"And you call me at the first sign of something wrong and I will come get you."

I thought about Grandma driving to Little Rock on her own. She probably could do it, but it would take her a three times as long as it should. She drives slower than the ferries that run through the French Quarter.

"Yes ma'am," I said again.

"You take care of yourself. And don't let all that mess Shelia does get to you. Okay?"

"Yes ma'am."

"You call me when y'all get in ya' hear?"

"Yes ma'am."

"Talk to you later. And don't you be down there acting crazy. I imagine you won't have much supervision."

"Yes ma'am."

Although I thought this call was coming to a close about three statements ago, clearly it wasn't. Grandma continued to talk. Reminding me to brush my teeth (like I'm ten years old), study, and that I had a concert next Friday with the school. I'm glad she brought that up; I hadn't told her that

I wasn't going to sing yet. She loves to hear me sing (she is the only one); I will be directing the choir. I have a good ear for music but not a good voice. I started to chime in and let her know, but decided that if I did, I would have to stay on the phone another thirty minutes and it sounded like she was wrapping up.

"Ocean!" she yelled.

"Ma'am," I replied.

"Chile you hear me talking to you?"

"Yes ma'am," I said.

"Well act like it then." Grandma expects a million yes ma'am's per conversation.

"Yes ma'am," I said.

"Well let me go. I got some gumbo on the stove I need to tend to."

"Okay. I will call you later."

Before I knew it she had hung up. My grandma is the only person I've never ended a telephone conversation with "I love you". She is not that type. Daddy says it doesn't mean she doesn't love; just that she is not big on expressing it.

I scrolled through my phone until I got to the text menu, then proceeded to check my messages. The first three were from Tisha. She said Tasha lived in a really nice house.

Judging from that information and the Benz she was driving earlier, I guessed grandma was right; Tasha clearly wasn't a college student. Tisha said she thinks she is dating a rich man. She also said that she had tried to call her mom several times but her cell phone was no longer working. I texted back and told her to have fun and not to worry, storms always mess with the cell phone service. I'm sure if Aunt Sheila had to rent a Cavalier, where I was going wasn't going to be quite as nice. I also told her to let me know as soon as she got a hold of her mom. I want her to watch out for grandma. I'm never comfortable when she is alone.

The last two texts were from Jovan. He was checking to see if we had made it to Little Rock. I wrote him back and told him that we were close.

Noticing that I was off of the phone, Aunt Shelia asked, "Can you drive?"

"Yes."

"Good. Cause I'm tired. We'll stop and fill up, and then you can take over."

Although I didn't really feel like driving, I figured it was best that I do so anyway. We stopped at the next exit, filled up and Aunt Sheila bought two 40 ounces of beer. If I had known she was going to start drinking, I would've told her I couldn't drive.

"You drink?" she asked as she twisted the cap from her first bottle.

"No."

"You have never drank at all?"

Actually, once Tisha and I drank with Charles and his college friends. I didn't like it though. Plus when I got home my grandma could smell it. I'm lucky she didn't tell my daddy, but she did make me promise that I would never do it again. So far I had held true to that promise. But I wasn't going to tell Aunt Sheila about that.

"No," I replied again.

"Is that the only word you know?"

"No," I replied sarcastically.

Before I knew it she had slapped me across my face with the back of her hand. Blood immediately gushed from my nose and I cupped my hands to catch it.

"Don't you talk crazy to me. We are going to nip this in the bud from the jump. You are not grown, and you will not talk to me any kind of way."

I didn't say a word. How could I? My nose was bleeding and I was still in shock that she had just hit me.

"You hear me talking to you?" she screamed.

I remained silent.

"I guess you need another one," she raised her hand and I jumped.

"That's what I thought," she said. "Now, I'm the only adult here. You hear me?"

"Yes ma'am," I mumbled through the hand full of blood.

"Now go clean yourself up."

I got out of the car and walked into the gas station. The attendant was busy with another customer. I was glad they didn't notice me. I hurried into the bathroom and let all the blood fall into the sink. I looked at myself in the mirror before I splashed my face with cold water and wiped it clean with a paper towel. My nose had stopped bleeding but my shirt was covered. After I dried my hands, I felt my pocket for my cell phone—I need to call Ms. Pitman and let her know, hurricane or not, I'm not staying with Aunt Crazy. Maybe I was a little rude to her, but she had no right to hit me. All my pockets were empty. I must have left my phone in the car.

What am I going to do? Where else can I go? After being in the bathroom for about ten minutes, I went back to the car.

Aunt Sheila had put on an old school blues CD and

was drinking her beer. I had it in my mind to take the bottle from her and hit her in the head with it, but that would just make things worse. I thought about my grandma and daddy. Daddy didn't need to be worrying about me and I didn't want to bother Grandma. If I told her what happened, her blood pressure would skyrocket. I decided I would just do the best I could to stay out of Aunt Sheila's way until I could get back to New Orleans.

Aunt Sheila didn't say a word to me. Just drank her beer and sang the songs from her CD. I drove the final two hours thinking about home and how I couldn't wait to get back there. I had no idea what Little Rock was going to be like. But if it was going to mean more back-hands and blood-stained shirts—I didn't want to find out.

Chapter Seven

"Hey baby girl." My daddy's voice coming from my cell phone made me feel five years old again.

"Daddy!" I exclaimed.

"Y'all make it to Little Rock yet?"

"Yeah," I said, wiping the sleep from my eyes. "What time is it?"

"Should be almost 9 a.m. there. What time did ya'll get in?"

It felt like I had been asleep a long time, but we had only been at Aunt Sheila's about an hour. "Around eight," I replied.

"How did momma handle the ride?" he asked. Oh no, I thought, he doesn't know.

I swallowed hard, then said, "Grandma didn't come, daddy."

"What? What do you mean she didn't come? I bought her a ticket too."

"Ms. Pitman got her to come to the station, even told her she would pack her stuff, but she refused to get on the bus. She said she would be okay."

"Ocean, how could you leave her? You know she's not in the best health. Why didn't someone try to call me?"

He sounded about as stupid as Aunt Sheila. He knew we couldn't call him while he is there, they can only call out. I really didn't know how to answer that without getting myself in some trouble.

"Don't worry daddy," I tried to comfort him, "She said she would leave with Ms. Pitman later."

"How much later? She don't need to be in New Orleans, Ocean. This is no thunderstorm!" He was almost yelling at me. Then I guess it must have hit him. "So you are with Sheila by yourself?"

"Yes sir," I replied.

"That is the last place I want you alone. I would rather you be anywhere. Momma knows you don't need to be with Sheila without her. She can be so stubborn sometimes."

I could hear the anger in his voice. I'm glad the conversation had switched from me to Grandma. I held the phone in silence. There was a long pause before he let out a sigh.

"I'm sorry baby," he said "It's not your fault. I just wish I was there. I can't sleep from worrying about you and momma."

"I wish you were here too Daddy." I started to cry.

"Come on Ocean. Don't do that," he said. "Are you still writing me letters?"

"Yes sir."

"They make you feel better?"

"Yes sir."

"Just keep writing baby. Like I've said so many times, that way you can talk to me anytime you want."

"I need you Daddy," I said, thinking about the backhand that Sheila had given me just hours earlier. If he was here, she wouldn't have thought about hitting me.

"I know baby. I don't want you there either. Let's just pray you'll be able to go back home soon. Right now, Sheila is our only option."

"You really think this hurricane is going to be bad?" I echoed Tisha's question to me. I hoped his answer would be as comforting as the one I gave, but it wasn't.

"I know it is baby. I can feel it."

He scared me. I started to worry about Grandma.

Daddy was right. How could I have left her behind? Why didn't I try to beg her to come? I could have cried or something. Instead I just stood there and did nothing.

"I'm sorry daddy. I shouldn't have left grandma."

"If it's one thing we both know, Momma is going to do what she wants to do. It's not your fault. Have you been keeping up with the storm?"

Aside from the coverage we watched in school, I hadn't seen a single report. "Not really," I replied.

"You should. Just turn on CNN. They are tracking it."

"Yes sir," I said then went into the living room and turned on the television. I sat down on the couch as daddy continued to talk.

"I am going to try and find Momma. Have you talked to Ms. Pitman since you left?"

"No sir. Tisha said she tried to call, but couldn't get through on her cell."

"Okay. Make sure you keep up with what's happening there. As soon as it's safe, I will get you back home."

"Yes sir."

"Love you Ocean."

"Love you too Daddy."

We hung up just as I read the caption going across the

bottom of the screen. "New Orleans Mayor Nagin will hold a press conference at 10 a.m. this morning." It's a little after nine. I can't wait to hear what he has to say. Maybe he'll announce that all is clear and I can go home. Please let that be what he says.

Chapter Eight

I had no idea when I hung up with my daddy that Sunday, August 28th, was about to be the first worst day of my life.

I sat motionless in front of the television screen as Mayor Nagin issued a mandatory evacuation for the city of New Orleans. I texted Tisha.

Are you watching the news?

Yes. I have been trying to call my momma all morning, but I can't get through.

How are they going to leave? Your mom told me she was waiting for the first so she will have some money.

I don't know. I'm scared Ocean.

Even though I'm the brave one, I had to admit how I felt this time. *I am too Tisha.*

You talk to Jovan?

No. He texted me during the drive. I wrote back, but he hasn't replied.

I can't get in touch with anyone. I tried calling everyone I know.

I read Tisha's words and my stomach tightened the way it did when I found out my daddy had to go to Iraq. I felt alone, confused and weak. The exact opposite of the resilient girl I had been all my life.

I will call you later, I wrote.

Somehow I had lost all my words. Guess they left with the hope I had before I heard Mayor Nagin say it was no longer safe for anyone to be in New Orleans. I buried my head in my hands. I didn't want to cry, but I did. After a couple of minutes, I went to get my backpack from the bedroom. I had to talk to my daddy. I flipped my notebook to a fresh page. I hadn't mailed the first letter, but he would just have to get two at the same time.

Daddy,

I'm so confused. Looks like your feelings were right. The mayor just issued a mandatory evacuation. I want to be strong, but not sure how to be. Everyone I love, except for you, is in New Orleans. Grandma, Ms. Pitman, Jovan—it hurts me to think about them. What about our home daddy? I feel so helpless. I have no one. Aunt Sheila doesn't say much that makes sense to me, so I don't talk to her. In fact, I hate her. What am I going to do if I have to stay here? I miss you Daddy. I miss Grandma, I miss New Orleans—I miss home...

Love,
Ocean

That's all I could write. What else was there to say? I closed my notebook and made a mental note to mail my letters. I stretched out on the couch and continued to watch television until I drifted off to sleep.

Chapter Nine

"Wake up girl! That storm done hit New Orleans!" Aunt Sheila was screaming as she was looking around the room for the remote. She found it on the coffee table where I left it the night before. "See," she said, changing the station. "It's on every channel!"

I jumped up from the couch and stood directly in front of the television.

"Winds in New Orleans are reported to be blowing at 145 miles per hour..." Aunt Sheila had stopped on a station and the commentator was talking. "Power lines are down; thousands are huddled in the Superdome. We can only hope that many took the mayors advice and evacuated the city..."

She continued to talk as I was frozen with shock. My

hands began to shake and my body felt weak. I grabbed my cell phone and pressed Tisha's number into the keypad. Each number seemed harder to press than the one before. It rang twice before Tisha picked up.

"Hello?"

"Tisha..." I cleared my throat so words could come out.

"Ocean!" Tisha cried out.

"Tisha," I said again. There was tightness in my chest. Holding the receiver in one hand, I stood up. I wanted to yell but there was a knot in my vocal cords. I tried to cry but my eyes were holding back.

"What if they don't make it Ocean?" Tisha was now sobbing.

I couldn't stand to think about that right now. I threw the phone against the wall and began to move frantically through out the house. "No, no, no," I repeated to myself. I went back into the living room and looked underneath the sofa.

"Ocean, just calm down now," Aunt Sheila said following behind me.

I raced to the bedroom where I'd fallen asleep earlier.

Where are my shoes? I asked myself. I've got to get out of here. Finally, I found them underneath the pants I'd worn on the ride. I pulled the low cut jeans on over the boy boxers I'd slept in, slipped into my gray tennis shoes and ran out of the door.

"Ocean!" Aunt Sheila yelled. "Where the hell are you going?!"

I didn't look back. I sprinted down the steps and up the block. With each step I took my heart raced faster and faster. I wasn't sure where I was going. I wasn't even sure who I was. I just knew that I needed to get away. I ran until my legs crumbled beneath me. Somewhere between a yellow brick house and an elementary school, I collapsed.

Chapter Ten

I opened my eyes to a bright light.

Once focused I could see a shower curtain like divider to my left and a young red headed woman looking through a cabinet to my right. The room was cold and smelled like my school cafeteria. I was confused. The last thing I remember was running through Shelia's neighborhood after I found out the hurricane hit.

I tried to speak, but my tongue was heavy. I swallowed hard then asked, "Where am I?"

"What did you say honey?" a thick southern accent asked.

I don't know why, but I couldn't get anymore words out. I guess the nurse must have taken note.

"Its okay baby, you just rest. I will get your regular nurse."

I felt a soft hand on my cheek, and then heard a door close. After about a minute or so, it became clear that I was in a hospital. Aside from the beeping of the machines I was connected to, the room was completely quiet. I used my arms to push myself up in the bed. Just as I was almost comfortable, the same nurse along with a new one, rushed to my side.

"Sweetheart, you need some help? Be careful," the new nurse said as they both assisted me.

I looked at the two women wondering why they thought I couldn't sit up in the bed. I'm not handicapped.

"Who are you?" I mumbled to the obviously older nurse. Actually, she reminded me a little bit of my grandma. Her grey hair was pulled back into a bun highlighting the wrinkles on her forehead.

"I am the same nurse from the past three days."

"Three days?" I asked. "What's today?"

"Today is Friday, September 2nd."

"What happened?" I asked

"You were brought in on Monday night. A lady found you face down in her yard. You had fallen and hit your head. You have a serious concussion, that's why you can't remember anything."

"I remember running," I said.

47

"You do? Well that's improvement; you couldn't recall a thing yesterday."

"Where is my cell phone?" Speaking of remembering, has anyone talked to my grandma?

"We still don't have a cell phone, sweety. Maybe your aunt will bring it to you when she comes."

"My aunt?" I asked.

"Yes, baby, your aunt," she replied like she was a brand new kindergarten teacher.

Aunt Sheila is the one person I wish I could forget. I just want to find my phone so I can figure out what's happening to my grandma. I'm sure Tisha has been looking for me. And I don't even know where Jovan is. I started to look around the room for my clothes.

"Sweetheart, can you tell me your name?" the nurse asked.

"Ocean."

"Do you know your last name?" she asked.

Why is she asking me these stupid questions? Of course I know my last name. I gave her a "please leave me alone" look. "Sims," I said.

Apparently, she wasn't reading my non verbals. "And when is your birthday?"

I ignored her question and continued to look around for my clothes. I have to get dressed, get out of here and find my phone.

"Ocean, honey, what are you looking for?"

Now she asked a relevant question. "My clothes."

"Why do you need your clothes?"

That didn't last long; she's back to dumb one. I ignored her again. I moved the cover from my legs and tried to swing them to the edge of the bed so I could stand up.

"Sweetheart, where are you going?"

Why is this lady talking to me like I'm an old woman with Alzheimer's? I thought. *Why won't she leave me alone?* I continued to try to get out of bed.

"Just lay down. Your aunt will be here shortly." She was pulling the cover back over my legs.

"I can't stay here," I said.

"Well why not?"

"Look, a hurricane just hit New Orleans and my grandmother is there."

"Honey, why don't you watch some television, you have been glued to it since you been here."

"I have?" I asked. I don't remember coming here, let alone watching television.

"Yes you have."

"What's wrong with me again?"

"You have a serious concussion. You are doing better though. Just need to give your head some time to heal, then your memory will return to normal."

"And I have been here for three days?"

"Yes."

"Does my daddy know?"

"You talked to him yesterday."

This must be bad. I don't remember a thing. Once Jovan got a concussion during a football game, but it didn't last three days. He was funny though, didn't even remember playing in the rest of the game. I took the nurses advice and turned on the television. At least I can find out what's happening in New Orleans. I relaxed and the nurse turned on the TV.

"You hungry?" she asked.

I looked up at the television screen. "No, I'm fine."

"Okay. You can use that remote next to your bed to change the channel. I'll be back in a little while."

I turned to CNN.

"President Bush doesn't care about black people," Kanye West said boldly with a look of disgust on his face. Then it cut back to the news reporter. "These controversial words were spoken by hip-hop artist Kanye West during a benefit concert for Hurricane Katrina relief efforts..." I hung on to every word she said. All those rappers out here claiming to be hard, but Kanye's words were the most gangsta thing I've ever heard.

"...Seems the rapper is upset by the government response in New Orleans. He, like many, feels that FEMA did not respond in a timely manner." Then I saw images of New Orleans for the first time since I was driven away on the bus.

My home looked like a small colony in a bottom of a fish tank. My people where floating on top of whatever they could find. Some were hanging from rooftops. Grown men were helpless, babies were crying, and everyone was begging. I felt guilty for leaving, like I should be there with my grandma, helping her through all of this. Instead, I'm stuck in a hospital bed, waiting for my memory to return. I wondered where Jovan was. Did he do like his coach suggested? Just when I thought I had seen the worst, they showed footage of the Superdome.

My memories of Saints games and concerts faded with the first image. There was a sea of people, some in complete panic. I watched closely, hoping to get a glimpse of someone I knew.

I couldn't believe what I'm seeing.

I blinked.

My heart screamed, and pain took over my chest. This was a whole new feeling, something I'm sure I never felt before. My eyes widened and I covered my open mouth with my hand. It always hurt me to see people in need, but this hurt was different because they were images of my home.

I sat alone once again with only my thoughts. What is happening to my life? My daddy told me once that a life full of sunshine is a miserable life, dry like the desert. He said we all need rain, it keeps us balanced.

But myself and New Orleans have had more rain in the past week than either of us could take.

Chapter Eleven

Where is she?

I am furious. I have been sitting in the bed for almost three hours waiting for Aunt Sheila. I need my cell phone. I pushed the button above the bed for my nurse.

"May I help you?" she answered.

"Will you call my Aunt again?" I asked.

"Sure. You need anything else?"

I thought for just a second.

"Paper and pen please," I needed to talk to my daddy.

"No problem."

I turned off the TV. I had seen all I could take for the day. Plus they keep calling us refugees and evacuees like we aren't American citizens. It was making me upset. A short time later, an elderly nurse came in with a yellow legal pad and a pen.

"This is the best I could do."

She handed me the pen and pad.

"Thanks," I replied.

"I called your aunt she said she would be here shortly. You are a lucky young woman."

Lucky? She clearly didn't know what was happening in my life.

"What do you mean?" I asked.

"Your aunt has spent every night here with you. I know because I'm the only one who works this shift."

She couldn't be talking about Aunt Sheila. I figured she would be happy to get rid of me. Maybe she felt guilty for hitting me. Who knows? And to be honest, I didn't care. The nurse took a seat on the edge of the bed.

"Ooh chile, these old feet done had it," she removed her shoes and rubbed her arches. "Thirty years, I've been a nurse at this same hospital. I will tell you something I've learned. We don't always understand the people in our life, but they are here for a reason."

I thought about her words. Could Aunt Sheila be in my life for a reason? If so, what is it? None of it makes sense to me. I guess the nurse could sense my confusion.

"It will be okay," she said. She gave me a pat on the leg, and then stood to leave.

Once she disappeared outside the door, I picked up the pen and pad...

Dear Daddy,

The tears came. I knew they would...

I'm so lost. Nothing is going right. I keep wondering if I will ever get back to the life I know. The one where there are no hurricanes or Aunt Sheila. The one where grandma fixes huge Sunday dinners with gumbo and crab legs. The one where I can see my best friend everyday and eat lunch with Jovan whenever I want. Daddy, I want to be home. I'm empty inside. I'm trying to find my way, but to be honest, I don't know where I'm going. I can't do this alone. I need someone. Daddy, I need you. Please come home.

Love,

Ocean

"Heyyy Ocean." I heard an extra happy voice. I looked up from my pad.

It was Aunt Sheila.

I could tell by her free-flowing body language that she was drunk. I wouldn't have said a word to her, but I was lying in a hospital and she had the nerve to come in drunk? I'd had enough.

"Don't hey me," I rolled my eyes. "I am sick of you treating me like crap. Since the day you picked me up, you haven't wanted me. Now you show up here drunk looking like a crack head. You know what? You can leave. I can figure this out on my own."

I turned over in my bed so that my back was facing her. I expected her to hit me again, but she didn't. Instead a few seconds passed and I heard her slide a chair next to my bed. She took a deep breath then said four words that nothing in this world could have prepared me for.

"Ocean, I'm your mother."

My Mother? I thought, how could she be my mother? I turned and looked her in the face.

When I was young I thought about the type of mother I wanted. I always imagined her dressed in an apron with curls in her hair. Instead, the woman who claims to be my mom is wearing a pair of 6 inch black stilettos and a skirt so short that when she crossed her legs I could see her panties. Her eyes matched the color of her bright red lipstick and her long blonde weave hung to the middle of her back. It looked like she hadn't combed it in days. She smelled of cigarettes and dark alcohol.

Her words were on repeat in my head. I'd heard them, but I don't believe them.

"Now I want you to listen to me," she slurred. "I have never in my life loved anyone the way I love you."

Really? I thought. Then why wait seventeen years to tell me this?

"When I had you," she continued, "I was young. Fifteen years old. And I was out of control. I was staying with Momma and Willie had just been stationed in New Orleans."

"Wait!" I had to interrupt. "Are you telling me that my daddy ain't my daddy?"

She started to cry, but quickly caught the tears with a bent forefinger before they reached her eyeliner. A few seconds passed before she looked up at me. Her gaze went far beyond my eyes. I felt as if she was staring into my soul. "No, Ocean," she said, "He's not. Willie is your uncle."

Her words wouldn't resonate. "I don't believe you," I said. "Why should I? My daddy and grandma would never lie to me. Plus you're drunk."

Aunt Sheila reached in her purse and retrieved a white

envelope, my cell phone and charger.

"The nurse said you wanted me to bring you these." She motioned with her head toward the electronics. "And I think you should have this now."

I took all three items from her hand. She swung her weave over her shoulder, and then stood to leave. I watched as she stumbled out of the hospital room just as drunk as she had come. I then looked down at the envelope she had given me. There, written in the most beautiful handwriting I'd ever seen, were the words:

For my daughter Ocean Renee Sims on your eighteenth birthday.

Chapter Twelve

I opened the envelope.

I had to.

As I unfolded the white notebook paper that was inside, an old Polaroid fell on my lap. I picked it up then held it close to my face. It was of a teenaged girl holding a newborn in a hospital bed. I couldn't tell who the girl was, but she was gorgeous. At the bottom of the picture was my birthday written in black marker, February 2, 1985. I looked back up at the image, this time with a detective's eye. Still neither face looked familiar to me. I decided to read the letter.

Ocean,

If you are reading this then you are 18 years old. I'm sure you have grown into a beautiful young woman. Momma and

*Willie wouldn't have it any other way. I am writing this letter
on the eve of your tenth birthday. For a decade of my life, February 1 has been the hardest day of the year. I think of the day in
1985 when I rode to the hospital in the front seat of my friend's
old Honda. He was panicking and I was in so much pain. I was
only in labor a short time. We got to the hospital at eight, and by
midnight I was holding you. Once I saw your face I knew it was
all worth it.*

    *Since you have been away from me, I feel that same pain,
the same time, every year. One day you will know our secret.
Just in case I'm not around when that time comes, I want you to
know my story—the one that I've tried to drown in alcohol for
ten years.*

    I stopped reading. I know that if I keep going, what I
will find out might change the only life I've known forever.
I'm not sure if I'm ready for that to happen. The hurricane
had destroyed enough. I want to hold on as long as I can. I
buzzed the nurse again.

    "Yes?" A voice came through the intercom; it was the
same nurse from before.

    "I would like to sit by the window."

    "I'll be right in."

A few minutes later she came into my room and moved the chair next to the window.

"You hungry yet?" She asked.

"Yes, I am."

"I'll find you some dinner."

"Thank you."

She moved next to my bed and started unplugging me from the machines. "You need anything else?"

I thought about it for a second, and then retrieved my daddy's letters from my bag. "Will you mail these for me?" I asked.

"I sure will baby. Just write down an address."

As I wrote down the mailing address she continued to prep me for my move. I wondered how long it would take my daddy to write me back. "You ready?" the nurse asked.

I looked up at her. "How long do you think I'll be in here?" I asked.

She didn't answer. Instead she started helping me to my feet. Once I was standing, she let me go.

I sat back down on the bed.

"What did you sit down for?" she asked.

"You let go."

"What? You think you can't make it on your own?"

I didn't know how to answer her question. I had tried to walk to the bathroom on my own, but had been unsuccessful.

"What's wrong chile?" she asked. "A cat got your tongue?"

"No ma'am," I replied.

"Well get up from there. Come on now."

She helped me stand again. This time when she let me go, I realized I had more strength than I thought did. After I took the first step, the others where easy.

The nurse laughed a prideful laugh. "That's it, chile. If you want to get out of this place, you have got to stand on your own."

Chapter Thirteen

I needed to clear my mind.

I sat for about ten minutes in front of the window with my head bowed, and said a soft prayer. I asked for strength and courage. It's obvious that the life I've known is over; and I am still in shock to find out about this new one. Is Shelia really my mother? I know her and my grandma don't get along, so maybe this is her way of trying to get me on her side.

When I finished my prayer, I picked up my cell phone to call Tisha. Once I powered it on, I saw that my voicemail box was full. I didn't have time to check them now. I found Tisha's number in my contacts and pushed talk.

"Ocean!" she yelled when she picked up. "Where have you been? I've left you a million messages!"

"Have you talked to your mom?" I asked. I heard her question, but we could get to me later.

63

"Nothing yet. But they are bringing people to Houston by bus, so Tasha and I have been at the drop off point every-day since they started."

"I'm really worried about my grandma," I said.

"I know. But I did see some old folks get off the bus today. Mrs. Washington is strong. Plus you know she know everybody. Somebody in the neighborhood looked out for her."

Tishas' words gave me a little hope. My grandma is a fighter. In fact she is the strongest woman I know. But after seeing what I had just seen on television, there was a small part of me that worried if she had survived.

"You're right," I said. I couldn't lose hope.

"Have you heard from Jovan?"

"I haven't heard anything aside from what I see on TV."

"Where have you been? I've been trying to find you."

"You won't believe the week I've had. The night the hurricane hit, I just couldn't take it. It's like my life was disap-pearing. I ran out of the house. And that's the last thing I remember. From what I was told, I fell and hit my head on a rock, and I've been in the hospital with a concussion three days."

"Oh wow. Three days? And you don't remember any of

them?"

"No. But the nurse said I was awake and everything."

"I've never heard of that before."

"Me either."

"Well, I haven't been in the hospital or anything, but the past week has been a big blur. I've been losing weight. Can't eat. Can't sleep. I stay glued to the television. I've called everyone I know. I made flyers with my mothers' picture. I just can't stop thinking about home."

"Judging from what I see, we won't be going back to New Orleans anytime soon," I said.

"I know," Tisha replied. "Tasha said I'm going to have to start school in another couple of weeks if things don't get better."

School? I hadn't even thought about going to school in Little Rock. But I guess I wouldn't have a choice.

"I haven't even thought about that," I said.

"Me either. Tasha brought it up. She said it was going to take awhile for New Orleans to be livable again."

"Guess I will have to start here too." I was so busy worrying about when I could go home that I hadn't thought about the possibility that I never would.

"How is it there?" Tisha asked. I started to tell her that

so far it has been pure hell. But she had enough on her plate than to be worried about me. And I couldn't tell her about Sheila claiming to be my mother. I hadn't even finished the letter.

"It is what it is," I said.

"It's not too bad here. I haven't done much of anything. But it's okay."

"Well maybe I can come there."

"I'm sure Tasha won't care."

"We'll see. Anyway," I said thinking about the letter, "let me get off here. I will call you later."

"Okay," Tisha replied.

We said our goodbyes, then hung up. I dialed my grandma's home number even though I knew I wouldn't get an answer. In fact it didn't even ring, just gave what sounded like a fast busy signal. I wanted to check my text messages next to see if I had gotten something from Jovan. But I knew it was time. I had to finish Aunt Sheilas' letter. I picked it up, and continued from where I'd left off.

Chapter Fourteen

I don't know how to begin. The story of my life is a compli-cated one that I think sometimes only I understand. Our whole life, Willie has been the good son, and me the prodigal daughter. I was always in trouble, grades were never good—I hung out with all the wrong people. By the time I was fourteen, Momma had had enough. So she sent me to here to Arkansas to live with your grandfather. It was cool at first, until I met your father. I loved his confident attitude. He was a freshman football player at the University of Arkansas. I lied and told him I was eighteen and had just finished high school. It didn't take long before I was basi-cally living in Fayetteville with him. My father had me emanci-pated and I didn't talk much to Momma or Willie. I thought I had it all figured out. There I was at fourteen, living a complete lie.

It didn't take long for the relationship to end. I found out that he had a girlfriend back in Texas where he was from. By the time all this happened, I was already a month pregnant with you. When I told him I was pregnant, he was excited for a little while until he went to Texas for a weekend. I'm not sure what happened from that point on, but apparently, I wasn't good enough anymore. When he returned he told me that he wanted nothing more to do with me until you were born. I packed my bags and I left. Every once in awhile, I would see him driving down the street in his purple Chrysler or read an article about him in the newspaper. But once I left Fayetteville and came back to Little Rock, he disappeared into my past. So there I was, fourteen, pregnant with no place to go.

I eventually met a woman at one of the halfway houses I lived in who said she could hook me up with a fake I.D. and get me a job as a waitress at a club. At three months I was barely showing, so I took her up on her offer. Before I knew it, I was making money. But the bigger I got, the more my boss kept saying that I had to leave until the baby came. At seven months, I was huge. He insisted that I had to go, but promised me my job back once I had you. I went to this place for pregnant teens and they took care of me for a month or so. I was still lying about my life. I told them I didn't know who your father was and my parents *were dead. Well it didn't take them long to figure out the latter was a lie. One day while I was asleep in my bed, Momma and Willie walked through the door.*

I must admit I was happy to see them. They had been looking for me since my father had me emancipated. I left and went back to New Orleans with them and two months later you were born.

I wanted to be the perfect mother.

I dressed you in the best clothes and each night before you went to bed I would sing to you. I wanted to be like the mothers on television, always there for you, holding you, loving you...

Ocean, believe me when I say my intentions were always good. At fifteen years old, I wanted to be a great mother, but I wasn't. I would leave you for days at a time with your grandmother; I had gotten into drugs and other things. Basically, I was still a teenager. Willie was more of a parent to you. Eventually the time came where Momma couldn't take anymore. She told me I had to get it together or leave her house. I chose to leave. I packed all of our stuff and was once again headed to Arkansas. Just as I was about to walk out of the door, Momma told me I could leave, but you weren't going anywhere.

At that moment I wanted to change my mind and stay, but my pride got in the way. I handed you over to my mother

Love, Ocean

*and walked out of the house. Since that day, I have been living
an empty life. I tried over the years to come back and get you,
but Momma and Willie filed for legal custody and won, but only
because I could not make it back to New Orleans for the court
day to fight for you. I didn't have the money to return.*

*Ocean, I know you will probably hate me once you read
this letter, but understand that I always loved you and I did what
I thought was best at the time. Please forgive me.*

*Your Mother,
Sheila Renee Sims*

I looked up from the letter and tried to process it all.
For some reason, something inside of me wouldn't let this
news touch my heart. The thought of Sheila being my mother
was ludicrous. I shifted my focus to finding out what was
happening with my grandma and Jovan. I stuck the letter in
between the pages of the legal pad the nurse brought me and
its contents in the back of my mind. I then picked up my cell
phone to listen to the messages. The first five were from Tisha.
She was trying to figure out where I was. The next three were
from my dad. I hadn't remembered speaking to him, but

his messages that said "I'm calling your cell like you asked" proved I had. I need to find a computer so I can send him an email and let him know that I'm feeling better.

The remainder of the messages were from Tisha as well. Still no word from Jovan or anyone back in New Orleans. I stretched my legs out one at a time before I stood up and made my way to the shower. After undressing, I stood completely underneath the flowing water. I wanted the water to wash away all the pain. It didn't, but at the very least it camouflaged my tears.

Chapter Fifteen

After about a ten minute shower, I dried myself, and then dressed in a clean hospital gown I found in the closet. I sat down on the edge of the bed and applied some lotion to my heel, then slid my feet into a pair of house shoes that were next to the bed. I took a deep breath then looked around the room. For the first time I noticed that there where fresh flowers sitting on the counter. I also had a brand new bottle of deodorant and other toiletries. Now that I think about it, the house shoes that were now on my feet didn't belong to the hospital. I stood and walked around to the other side of the bed to see if there was a card on the flowers—there wasn't. They had to have come from Aunt Sheila. I don't know anyone else in Arkansas.

I pushed the page button for the nurse. A few seconds

later she answered.

"May I help you?"

"Is there a public computer here I can use?" I asked.

"It sure is. On the seventh floor at the end of the hallway."

"Thanks," I said, hoping I could catch my daddy on line.

I took one last look at the flowers, still no card, and then headed out of the door into the hallway. It took awhile for my eyes to adjust to the bright lights and my legs were still a little shaky, but other than that I felt fine. I moved passed several other patients' rooms, careful not to look in. I figured they didn't want me all in their business. Before long I made it to the front desk.

"Ocean," a male nurse said when he saw me.

"Yes."

"Where are you going? You are not supposed to be out of bed."

"I'm going to the computer room," I replied, praying he wouldn't send me back to my room.

"Are you sure—"

Before he could finish his statement, my regular nurse came around the corner. "Leave that chile alone," she said, "If you had been through what she been through, you would be on the internet trying to find your family too."

He did just what she said and I continued to the elevator.

"You make sure you be careful," she said.

"Yes ma'am," I replied just as the elevator opened.

I stepped inside and pushed the button for the seventh floor. The elevator smelled like latex gloves and scented Vaseline. I stared in the huge mirror that was in the back of it. There were bags under my eyes and I needed to find a comb quick. I guess I hadn't thought much about physical appearance since I left home. I stared closely at my dark brown skin examining it for breakouts. I used to do this every morning. Grandma always said that if you treat pimples early, they won't be so bad. I didn't see any. I also took a good look at my teeth. They were still the same. Perfect, except for the small gap in the front. When I was younger, I thought it was ugly, but I have learned to accept it as a part of me, plus Jovan doesn't have a problem with it. I re-did my ponytail, hoping I could at least make my hair look a little better. Just as I stretched my rubber band one last time, the doors slid open revealing a tall handsome teenage boy. He glanced at me for a second with huge half dollar sized eyes, then moved to the

side so I could exit. Under different circumstances I would
have stopped to talk, but I had a boyfriend and too much
happening in my life to be making friends. I turned my body
to the left, careful not to touch the boy, and exited the elevator.

The seventh floor was just like the tenth floor I was
on, except there were no nurses sitting at the desk. I looked
around for a sign that would tell me where the computer lab
was. There wasn't one. I decided to go to the right. I walked
down the hallway until I spotted a janitor.

"Excuse me," I said.

The old man looked up from the floor he was mopping.

"Can you tell me where the computers are?" I asked.

He didn't say a word. Just pointed down the hallway in
the direction I was headed. I continued until I got to an area
that had five computers set up and several televisions with
video games. I sat down in the first empty seat and wiggled
the mouse. As the page loaded, I prayed they already had instant messenger downloaded. When all the icons appeared on
the desktop, I was happy to find that they did. I clicked the
happy face and logged in.

Although I had no friends online, I scrolled to my
father's name and started a conversation anyway.

Hey Daddy, I typed. *Got ur mess. I maild ur ltrs 2day. Writ me bak wen u get ths! Luv U!*

I hit the enter key then minimized the screen, and logged on to MySpace. As my page loaded, I saw that I had new messages in my inbox. Before I checked them, I scrolled down to my top friends list and navigated to Jovan's page. I knew that if it said he had logged in recently, then he was safe. It took awhile for his page to load. I could hear his song long before I could see his picture.

I started to cry just listening to the lyrics. Jovan loves Lyfe Jennings and had chosen "Must Be Nice" for his page. I couldn't help but think how anything would be nice for me right now. Finally Jovan's profile loaded and to the left of his picture it read: Last log in August 28, 2005, the day Mayor Nagin had issued the mandatory evacuation. My tears flowed harder. I scrolled down to his friends list and started to click on other classmates' profiles. They all said the same thing. There were no updates, no newly written comments, no new bulletins. Nothing. MySpace was dead. I could only pray that the people behind the profiles were not.

Finally my MySpace search was ended by the cartoon like sound that IM makes signaling a new message. I quickly navigated back to the IM screen.

Baby Girl you still there? It was my father—always on time.

Yes I'm here, I typed as fast as I could, then struck the enter key.

I'm so worried about you. I'm trying to come home. Are you okay?

Yes sir. I'm fine. U thnk thy are goin to let u cum home?

They don't have a choice. I will go awol if I have to. Are you still in the hospital?

Yes sir.

Is Sheila taking good care of you?

Yes sir. I guess she is. She had brought everything I needed to the hospital.

I've been reading the reports about the hurricane on CNN's web page. Things are really bad there.

I know. People are dying daddy. Not just a few here and there, but lots of people. It's hot, no electricity and it seems like no one is helping. I'm scared for Grandma. I just wish I would have stayed behind with her.

It's not your fault, Ocean. It's no ones fault.

I know. I just wish there was something I could do.

There is something.

Really? I typed. Maybe my father knows something I

don't.

You can be strong, full of hope and beat life's hardships, rather than letting them defeat you.

I'm trying to be strong. It's just so much.

I'm not saying it's easy, only that it's nothing that you can't handle. And more than that, nothing that you can't handle on your own.

My father's words scared me. I didn't know what to reply. Instead I stared blankly at the computer screen. Seconds later my dad sent another message.

Ocean, you are seventeen years old. I have taught you right from wrong and how to take care of yourself. Right now you have to show me that I have done a good job. Show the world that nothing can stop your greatness. Success for you is inevitable.

I studied his words. I hadn't even considered that in the midst of all the drama in my life, I could still be great. Just a month ago, I was downloading college applications and taking ACT prep courses. I wanted to attend Fisk College and major in music. I had forgotten that I once dreamed of directing a choir at one of the big arenas I'd seen on TV. I had forgotten that my grades had improved drastically this year. I was proud of my 3.5 g.p.a. It was a huge step up from the 2.5 I ended my sophomore year with.

Baby... my daddy typed.

Yes sir? I responded.

This hurricane may have changed your life, but it doesn't have to change your dreams.

I read his words, then smiled the first smile I'd had in awhile. I felt a sense of peace flow through my body. I relaxed into my chair and typed the words, *Now that you are there, I really do have the best daddy in the world.*

Chapter Sixteen

I'm out of here.

My daddy's words were all I needed to get up and start living again. I spent yesterday waiting for the doctor to release me. Since I only had a concussion, I was free to leave once my memory came back, I had no problems yesterday. I still don't remember the days after I hit my head, but everything else is back to normal.

Oddly enough, I still wasn't let go until this morning, Sunday, September 4, the same day that the last of my people were rescued from the Superdome. I watched all the reports closely. Still no sight of Grandma, Jovan or Ms. Pitman. Tisha and I had texted more than we talked. She hadn't heard anything either.

I stood to the left side of the bed humming a tune and

dressing myself in a canary tee and dark jeans. It was my favorite outfit. I'd worn it on the first day of school and Jovan told me I looked beautiful. Since then, I felt like a princess every time I put it on.

I slipped into my yellow flip flops and then continued to pack my things back into my suitcase Aunt Sheila brought to the hospital for me. Just as I was getting ready to zip it up, Aunt Sheila walked through the door.

"You ready?" she asked with a smile.

"I have never been more ready," I said.

"Okay. I just met with the doctor; he said you should be fine."

"I feel fine," I said just as she picked up the suitcase from the bed.

I followed her out of the door. We made a quick stop at the nurses' station so she could sign some papers, and then headed toward the elevator. There was a stiff silence between us. I still didn't know what to think about the letter she had given me, and to be honest, I didn't want to think about it. I wondered if she would ask me about it, I hope not.

Minutes later I was riding down Interstate 630 in Little Rock in the passenger side of an Old Chevy. I hope she doesn't ask me to drive this thing. It's huge and from what

I could tell, not very reliable. We were headed back to her house on Jackson Street. As we drove into the neighborhood, there were teenagers standing on almost every block. When we got to Aunt Sheila's street, the guys from next door were playing dominoes and drinking underneath the tree in the front yard. I guess I'd never seen her neighborhood this time of day and it had much more life than I remembered.

"Home sweet home," Aunt Sheila said, putting the car in park.

Before I could reply, one of the guys from the yard yelled, "Where my money at Sheila?"

"Imma get it to you when I get my check," Aunt Sheila yelled back as the guy started toward us.

"You better quit playing with me."

"I'm not playing. Imma get it to you."

They were now standing face to face. I'd never seen Aunt Sheila so passive. For just a second she seemed afraid.

"What up Shawty. Yo peeps a'ight?" The guy reached his hand toward me.

I took his hand, and then we gave a half hug as I said, "I'm not sure. Still no word."

"Well welcome to Little Rock. You ought to come slap some bones wit' us later."

"That's what's up," I replied. My daddy is an Army man. They play dominoes all the time. So of course he taught me. Before he left, we played almost every night. I wouldn't mind getting on the table, plus any man who can scare Aunt Sheila is a friend of mine.

"We'll be right here all night. Come kick it wit us."

"Okay," I said before Aunt Sheila spoke again.

"Imma get that for you, Dre, for real."

"You better," he replied, then walked back to his own yard.

Aunt Sheila grabbed my bag from the trunk and we went up the stairs to the house.

Before I could get in the door good, she said, "You got school in the morning."

In the morning, I thought. I figured I could at least wait a week.

"So you ain't got time to be playing dominoes and carrying on." She dropped my bags on the living room floor.

"Can I wait until next Monday to start school? What if I get to go home?" I asked. In reality, I knew she was being devious and for whatever reason, didn't want me playing dominoes.

"What home?"

I said nothing. I'm just glad I didn't fall for her falla-
cious "nice aunt" routine she put on in the hospital. I should
have given her a treat and patted her on the head for doing
such a good job pretending. I didn't care what the letter said,
this trick ain't my momma. I turned my back to her, rolled
my eyes and went into the bedroom.

"You may as well get used to this place," Aunt Sheila
said, following me. "And you better keep this place clean. I
ain't no maid."

Whatever, I thought. I'm going home.

"You hear me talking to you?" she snapped.

"Yes ma'am," I said.

"Then act like it."

Lucky for me, she left the room after that, mumbling
something about needing a drink. A few seconds later I heard
the refrigerator door open, and then the sound of ice cubes
being dropped in a glass. Maybe she'll drink herself to sleep, I
thought.

I decided to listen to some music as I looked for something to wear to school. After getting my iPod from my bag,
I pushed one headphone in my ear and let the other hang. I
had to keep one ear open. I took heed to what Grandma said,
I was going to watch Shelia very closely. I sang along with Ali-

cia Keys, just listening to her helped to keep my mind off all that's happening in my life. Music does that for me. It takes me to a peaceful place. So far Alicia had helped me cope with my daddy going to Iraq and she had even gotten me through some tough times with Jovan. I'm sure she won't let me down this time.

I rumbled through the few pieces of clothing I brought. I mixed and matched, trying to find a good combination. After about fifteen minutes, I gave up and started packing my things back into my bags. I figured I'd just wear what I had on now. I'd only worn it back to Aunt Sheila's from the hospital.

I took off the outfit, hung it neatly in the closet and dressed myself for bed. I paused for a second in front of the mirror that was attached to the back of the closet door. I almost didn't recognize myself. I had lost some weight. I turned to the side and glanced back at my butt before I faced front again. Last year I begged daddy for a belly button ring. Of course he said no, but I still wanted one. Maybe that will be my eighteenth birthday present to myself.

Finally, I put on one of Jovan's football t-shirts. He gave it to me homecoming last year. When I sleep in it, it makes me feel close to him. Although it was early, I laid down in the bed. Pretty soon, I was thinking of Jovan as Ms. Keys sang me to sleep.

You give me butterflyz...

Chapter Seventeen

An hour later, my cell phone rang. At first I thought I was dreaming because it was Jovan's ring tone, but when I saw his face flash across the screen, I sprung from the bed.

"Jovan!" I screamed into the telephone. My heart was racing faster than an Olympic runner. "I'm so glad you're safe. Where are you?"

"Baton Rouge. Baby, it was crazy. You won't believe the stuff I saw."

"Was it as bad as they showed on TV?"

"Worse. I saw babies floating in the water. I did all I could to help, but I felt so weak. I still don't know where half of my family is."

"I haven't heard from Grandma."

"I tried to look for her in the Superdome, but there

87

were so many people it was impossible to find anyone."

"Who are you with in Baton Rouge?" I asked.

"The coaches at LSU put me up. Looks like I may have to finish my senior year here."

"Aunt Sheila just told me I will have to go to school tomorrow. But as soon as it's safe to return, I'm gong home."

"I feel you on that one. I wish I could go back. But after talking to the coaches, it might be best for me to finish here. Can you imagine how things will be in New Orleans? No one'll be interested in finishing a football season."

"Well, I guess I'll be alone, but I can't stay here with Sheila."

"She can't be that bad."

"You just don't know. You may have to make room for me in Baton Rouge."

"Fa' Sho'. You know I got you."

"I may have to take you up on that. I miss you."

"I miss you too boo. I tried all I could to call you. But the towers were down. I didn't get service until I got into Baton Rouge. And then my battery was dead. So I just got a chance to call."

"Ocean," Aunt Sheila yelled from her bedroom.

"Yes," I responded.

"You need to get off that phone; you got school in the morning."

I didn't reply. I didn't listen either.

"What did she say?" Jovan asked

"She told me I need to get off the phone."

"It's early."

"Now you know why I have to leave here. She's crazy."

"Listen, I don't want to get you in trouble; I'll call you when I wake up in the morning."

Before I could reply, the door of my room flung open.

"Did you hear what I said?" Aunt Sheila yelled.

"I'll let you go," Jovan said. "I love you Ocean."

"Love you too," I said, then hung up the phone.

As soon as I pushed the off button, Sheila grabbed me by the neck of my shirt and pulled me off of the bed.

"When I tell you to do something, you best listen," she said. The alcohol from her breath made my nose hairs stand up. How had she drunk so much so quickly? "If you looking for someone to feel sorry for you, you came to the wrong place. You ain't the only one dealing with stuff. She was my momma."

I closed my eyes and swallowed hard. What did she mean she *was* her momma? Was she implying that my grandma is dead? I balled my fist so tightly in my hands that my nails dug into my palm. My heart was telling me to just hit her as hard as I could and pray I knocked her out with one blow. Then grab my suitcase and get wherever I can the best I can.

Then I remembered what my daddy told me about making emotional decisions. He always says that the heart is a great place to store love, but when it comes to anger, you should always use your head. I opened my lids slowly and took a deep breath. "Yes, ma'am," I said. She'd better be glad my daddy taught me better.

She pushed me back to the bed. "Go to sleep," she slurred before staggering out of the doorway.

I sat on the bed letting what had just happened soak in. After a minute, I remembered my call from Jovan and a smile stretched across my face. He was safe. And who cares what Aunt Shelia thinks, maybe my grandma is too. For that I'm happy, and at that moment no one could take that from me, not Aunt Sheila or her alcohol.

Chapter Eighteen

Jovan called me! I texted Tisha from underneath my covers. Aunt Sheila may have been able to hear me talking, but let's see if she could here me texting.

What?! I still haven't heard a word from my man. Tasha says we are going to drive to New Orleans next weekend after everything is clear.

I'm going, I wrote.

How?

I don't know yet, but I will make it to Houston somehow.

That's what's up! I will let Tasha know.

I have to find my Grandma.

I know, right. My Uncle called yesterday, told us that he talked to my momma right before the storm hit and she told him she was going to try and ride it out. But that was before the man-

datory evacuation.

    Jovan said he looked for Grandma at the Superdome, but there were so many people he couldn't find her.

    I don't think your grandma would have gone there.

I read Tisha's words, and she was right. My grandma would have stayed in her house. Since it was in the lower Ninth Ward, I know it flooded. All the newscast said it was one of the first areas to get hit. But regardless, I wouldn't give up hope. I couldn't.

    You are probably right, I wrote back.

    What day are you going to try to get to Houston?

    What day do ya'll plan on leaving?

    Tasha said Friday evening.

    I'll be there before then.

    Can't wait to see you.

    Me either Tish. I'm about to text Jovan. I'll call you before school in the morning.

    School? I thought you were in the hospital.

    I got out today.

    And you are going to school tomorrow?

    Sheila is making me.

    She is evil.

    Tell me something I don't know.

Tasha told me I should start thinking about it, but I could wait until we know for sure whether I can go home or not.

Well, Sheila is making me go in the morning.

That sucks. But I'm sure you'll make the best of it. Just pretend I'm there with you.

I'll be okay. It'll give me some time to start planning how I'm going to get to Houston.

Okay. Be careful. You know me and Tasha will help. Just let us know.

Okay.

As I scrolled through my phonebook making my way to Jovan's number, I thought about what I was going to do. I had to get to Houston, and I knew I had to do it without Aunt Sheila knowing. Although she may have wanted to get rid of me, I couldn't take the chance of her being against it and making sure I didn't go.

Baby, are you asleep? I had selected Jovan's name and was sending him a text. It didn't take him long to reply.

Nope. What's up with your aunt?

I blame it on the alcohol.

That's crazy. You talked to your pops?

Yep. Instant messenger when I was in the hospital.

Hospital? For what?

Aunt Sheila made us get off the phone so fast earlier; I hadn't even gotten the chance to fill him in on what was going on with me.

The night the hurricane hit, I flipped out. I was so worried about everyone, you, Grandma, Mrs. Pitman... I ran out of the house and fell down and hit my head. The doctor says I had a panic attack that ended with a concussion.

How long were you there?

Almost a week. You won't believe what else happened.

What?

Shelia, gave me a letter...

What's so bad about that?

I thought for a second before I replied. Did I want to tell Jovan what is happening? I hadn't told Tisha, but the truth is, there is a lot that I tell Jovan that I don't share with Tisha.

Without giving it another thought, I texted back, *She says she is my mother.*

What? How?

Says she had me young, and my daddy and grandma ended up with custody, it's a long story.

Do you believe her?

I don't know. I don't want to.

94

Why not?

What do you mean why not? I don't want her to be my momma. She's crazy.

True dat. I haven't even met her and I think so too.

What am I going to do?

Can you get to Baton Rogue?

Tisha said she and Tasha are driving to New Orleans next weekend. I'm trying to get to Houston, and then maybe after we leave New Orleans they can drop me off there.

I want you with me. I'm living with a cool family here. They know all about you.

As I read his text, I realized how happy I am to be with Jovan. He loved me for me. I mean, he is popular, the star of the football team and could have any woman he wanted, but he chose me. He never pressured me to have sex, although it seemed everyone was doing it and he was not a virgin to say the least. He loved me and more than that, he respected me. He's the only man in my life I love just as much as I do my father.

I will get there, I wrote confidently, although I had no clue as to how.

I hope so. Your father made me promise to take care of you while he was away, I can't let him down.

Sounds like him. Always looking out for me.

You know that! He wants nothing but the best for you. I hope I'm a father like he is. I think about what life would be like if I had a father.

I used to think the same thing. What would life be like if I had a mother.

You got your grandma though; I have no one but my big bro.

You got me baby, I texted. It flowed so naturally that I knew it came from my heart. I'm sure I never had any doubts about loving Jovan, but if there were any they were all gone. I'm all in.

I know baby. You get some sleep. Call me tomorrow.

As soon as I wake up.

Okay. Goodnight.

Goodnight.

I turned over on my side and cuddled next to my pillow. There was nothing about my life that's in Little Rock. I didn't know how I was leaving, but I was. I would go to school in the morning like Sheila wanted, but Friday she'd be looking for me no doubt.

Chapter Nineteen

The next morning Aunt Sheila pulled up in front of Hall High School, then looked at me. I waited for her to turn off the engine. When she didn't, I got the hint but decided to ask anyway.

"Aren't you coming in?"

She had flipped down her visor and was applying her bright red lipstick. "I gotta go to work. It ain't like you a little girl."

I exited the vehicle with all attitude. What am I supposed to do? I didn't even know her address. I slammed the door shut. I was so sick of her. She was the most selfish person on the planet.

"Ocean," Aunt Sheila called after me.

What now? I thought. I turned around "Yes?"

She reached into her purse and handed me a folded

sheet of paper. "I wrote down my address and phone number in case you need it." She must have read my mind. I took the information and walked up the steps to the building. When I reached the front door, I took a deep breath before I entered. "Daddy, I know you are with me," I said, then pushed open the metal door.

The front lobby area looked nothing like my high school in New Orleans. It was a little less modern than what I was used to. There was a large trophy case directly in front of me and a security desk to the left. The small area was full of kids going each direction. I stopped for a second and took a look around. Judging from the paint on the walls, the school colors must be orange, white and navy blue.

"You lost?" a petite Hispanic girl asked me.

"Umm..." I hesitated. "I'm new, just trying to find the office I guess."

She pointed to the sign that read "office" which was right above the door to my left. I was so busy checking out the orange and blue wall I didn't bother looking in that direction.

"It's okay," the girl said. "I've been here a year now and I still get lost."

As soon as the words left her lips, a tall African American chick came up behind her and hit her right in the top of the head with her fist. My first instinct was to help her; I mean why would this big girl be hitting on someone so small? But before I could get in the middle of something that had nothing to do with me, the little Latina had spun around and pushed the bigger girl so hard she crashed into the trophy case.

"You must be loco. I'm not afraid of you!" she screamed. By this time, other students had come to see the action. I moved out of the way, but was still able to see.

"Bitch!" the big dark girl screamed while running back toward the other student. Her weave ponytail was barely holding on and from the looks of things she should have been running the other way. The girl I was talking too didn't look like a novice. You could tell by the way she snatched off her earrings this wasn't her first fight.

As soon as the big girl was in arms reach, she caught five quick blows to the face from much smaller fists. She managed to connect on one of her own punches but that made the girl I was talking to even more upset. She launched toward her and helped her weave make it to the ground. The crowd laughed and finally the security guards were able to get through and break up the fight. I must admit it was the most exciting thing I had seen since I left New Orleans.

Both girls continued screaming obscenities at each other as they were dragged into the office. The big girl looked like she had just walked out of a haunted house while the smaller chick was still put together like she had just finished dressing for school. She had a look of victory on her face. She knew she'd won.

"Sit!" A tall red head man yelled at the two girls who were now inside the office and being made to take a seat. "This stops here or both of you are expelled!" he yelled.

"But Mr. Graves, she hit me for no reason," the Hispanic girl snapped.

Of course that triggered a whole new yelling match. I was still standing outside the office watching and listening through the glass window.

"Gabriella, that's enough," the man said, ending the match again.

Gabriella, I thought. I like that name. And it fits her well. She looks like a Gabriella. At least she does to me. She is small and petite. If she had another foot of height, she could be a supermodel easy. Not only is she beautiful, judging from the way she walked up to me, she is confident as well.

"But Mr. Graves, I wasn't doing nothing to nobody.

She came out of no where and just hit me. Ask her," she said, pointing her finger dead at me.

"Come here young lady," he demanded.

I did as I was told.

"What's your name?" he asked.

"Ocean Sims," I replied.

"Are you new?"

"Yes sir."

"What class are you supposed to be in?"

"I don't have a class. It's my first day."

"Have you talked to anyone yet?"

"No sir."

"Did you see this fight?"

I didn't know what to say. Where I'm from, if you saw it, you didn't tell. That was snitching. I ain't no snitch.

I guess Mr. Graves, as Gabriella called him, could tell I was in an awkward position.

"Mrs. Cyr," he said, turning to the secretary. "Can you help this young lady get enrolled?"

He pointed me toward the front desk and went into his office. Seconds later, an older woman with perfect posture asked, "May I help you?"

"I'm a new student," I said softly.

"Where are you from?" She asked.

"New Orleans."

"Mrs. Jones, our counselor, is dealing with the Hurricane Katrina students." She handed me a clip board. "Fill this out, and I will find her for you, okay?"

"Yes ma'am," I replied, then took a seat, right in the middle of Gabriella and Goliath. (I wasn't sure what her name was, but I imagined she felt like Goliath, the giant that was slayed by David in the Bible, with only a sling shot).

Goliath was still very upset. She sat with her arms folded across her chest and her lips poked out. Gabriella, on the other hand, seemed quite serene with her victory. You could tell because she had taken out her compact and was freshening up her make up.

I looked down at the clipboard and filled in the blanks I knew. The truth is I didn't know much. They asked what classes I had already taken toward my high school diploma and my cumulative grade point average. I knew that I had a 3.5 so far this year, but we hadn't even gotten an official report card. I filled in my class schedule from home, but left most of the form blank. It didn't really matter. I was only going to be here a week. I did write down, though, all of the information from the paper that Aunt Sheila gave me. When

I came up missing, maybe they'd arrest her.

"Gabriella," Mr. Graves called as he stuck his head from his office door.

She stood up, walked past me and the other girl, who didn't dare look up. *At least she's smart*, I thought. No sense in getting two beat downs in one day. I continued to look at my form when I felt my phone vibrating in my pocket. I got it out to see it was an international call. That only meant it was one person...Daddy.

I put down the clipboard, stepped outside the office, and answered my phone.

"Daddy," I said.

"Hey baby girl. Where are you?"

"At school."

"School? Where?"

"In Little Rock. Sheila made me come."

"When did you leave the hospital?"

"Yesterday."

"And she made you go to school today?"

"Yes sir."

"How do you feel about it?"

Sometimes I think Daddy should be on TV like Dr. Phil. He always asks how I'm feeling and gives the best advice.

"I was mad at first, because we don't even know if I will have to stay here."

"So you are cool with it now?"

I thought about my plan to leave. "Yes," I said.

"Okay. So long as you're happy. Let me talk to Sheila."

"She didn't come in with me. Just dropped me off."

"What?" I could hear the anger in his voice. "Don't worry, I will be home soon, just waiting on some paper work."

"How soon?" I asked excitedly.

"Not sure, I will give you details once I know. What the hell is wrong with Shelia?"

I didn't reply. I figured he was venting and didn't want an answer.

"Baby Girl, let me call you back. I need to use this time to straighten some things out."

"Okay," I said.

"Have a good first day at school."

"I will."

"Love you."

"Love you too."

I shoved my phone in my pocket and went back into the office. Gabriella had come back and Goliath was gone.

"There you are," the secretary said. "Ms. Jones is in her

office. You know how to get to the media center?"

I handed her back the clipboard. "No ma'am," I said.

"I'll show her," Gabriella chimed in. "I have to go there next anyway."

The next thing I know, I was walking down the hall, getting an earful about the basis of the whole fight from loquacious Laquisha, which is what my English teacher in New Orleans called the girls who talked all the time.

"Can you believe she ran up on me like that? Like I was supposed to run? She got me bent. I ain't scared of no one..."

Gabriella was talking a million words per minute. I'm surprised she didn't pass out from lack of breathing. I listened to the story about how Nerica (that's the girl's name, guess it sounds better than Goliath) thought she was messing with her man, when really her man was trying to get at Gabriella.

"I tell you one thing, she won't ever run up on me again. The bigger they are the harder they fall. And guess what? I didn't even get suspended. I'm in-school suspension for three days but that's nothing..."

Why does she think I care about her drama? I thought. *Didn't she know that I have enough going on in my own life? Where is this counselor's office?*

"Yall got cute boys in New Orleans?" Gabriella asked. I

heard her say something about New Orleans, but I had tuned her out about 30 seconds ago.

"You hear what I said?" she asked.

"I'm sorry, what now?"

"I said do y'all have cute boys in New Orleans?"

"I guess," I replied. I wasn't trying to be rude, but I don't want to talk about cute boys or anything else for that matter. I just needed to get to the counselors office, so I could do whatever to get registered and then plan my escape.

"I bet y'all do. Lil' Wayne is fine and he's from New Orleans..." Gabriella had started with yet another monologue, this time about all the New Orleans rappers. She even talked about Master P on Dancing with the Stars. I was happy when I saw the media center and a sign that read, Linda Jones, Guidance Counselor.

Chapter Twenty

This wasn't an ordinary counselor's office.

I could tell by the decor that I had just walked into the office of someone who cared about her students and loved her job. After showing me where the office was, Gabriella told me she had to go to the bathroom. I was relieved to have some peace and quiet.

Mrs. Jones wasn't in her office, so I looked at the bulletin board full of pictures while I waited. There where all kinds of photos from every major school event. It made me think about the fact that I wouldn't be attending Benjamin Franklin's senior prom with Jovan, although we'd been planning that event for over a year. I had to stop looking; the photos were making me sad. I was just about to take a seat in one of the chairs in front of her desk when I saw another bulletin board that was covered with mug shots. I noticed instantly that all but three were black males. I stood looking at the pictures until I heard a voice say, "Those are all my babies who are in prison."

I turned and to my surprise was standing face to face with a short white woman with blond hair and glasses. I just expected that Mrs. Jones would be black. Almost every photo on the wall was of a black student.

"They are all very smart men," she continued, "just made such poor decisions. He"—she walked toward the bulletin board and pointed to one picture—"was a straight A student. He was on track to go to college on a full scholarship."

"What happened?" I asked.

"Wrong place at the wrong time, I guess. I still ask myself that same question."

We both stood for a second looking at the mug shot. He was a handsome guy. He didn't look like he could do anything wrong.

"Now," Mrs. Jones said, "how may I help you?"

"Umm, I'm Ocean Sims. The secretary told me to come see you."

"Are you new?"

"Yes ma'am. I'm from New Orleans."

"I understand. What grade are you in?"

"I'm a junior."

"I have to ask this, so don't think I'm crazy, but do you have any school records with you?"

"No ma'am."

"It's okay. We've had several students from New Orleans and no one had anything. So tell me what classes where you taking at home?"

I ran down my schedule as Mrs. Jones typed some things into her computer. Before long, she had printed a document and was looking it over.

"I think this may work for you," she said. "We will try it out. If you feel uncomfortable within any of these classes, let me know." She handed me the paper. As I looked it over, she continued to ask me questions.

"So who are you living with here?"

"My aunt."

"How is that working for you?"

"It's good," I lied. It didn't matter because I wouldn't be here long.

"Where did you go to school in New Orleans?"

"Benjamin Franklin."

"I don't think we've gotten any other students from

there. But there are about six others so far. I can imagine the number will grow over the next couple of weeks. Would you be interested in meeting some of the other students?"

"No thank you," I replied.

"Okay, well, I'm here if you need anything."

"Yes ma'am," I said.

"We are in third period right now. I'll have Gabriella show you where you're supposed to be."

I stood up and walked toward the door.

"Ocean," Mrs. Jones said before I left. "My door is always open."

Her statement made my heart smile.

Chapter Twenty One

I felt like an Arab in the airport when I walked into my third period class. There was a girl up front showing more of her chest than I cared to see and another popping her gum more than I cared to hear. I suddenly felt uncomfortable in my baby tee and hip hugging jeans.

"This is Ocean Sims," Ms. Finley, the teacher, said. "She will be joining us for the rest of the year."

That's what she thinks, I thought.

"Ay yo, you was in that hurricane?" a voice from the back of the room said.

Before I could shake my head, the teacher said, "Yes, she was a part of the tragedy in New Orleans, I'm sure she will talk about that when she's ready. Until then, let's refrain from asking her questions." She gave me a June Cleaver smile and suggested I sit in the front seat.

I hate the front seat, but I sat down anyway.

The teacher went back to the front of the class. "Where were we?" she asked.

"*We* was about to fall asleep," the same voice said again and everyone laughed.

"It's we *were*, and that was a rhetorical question."

"And I gave you a *rhetorical* answer."

I finally turned to see where the voice came from. There in the last seat of the 3rd row sat a boy with short dreads and smooth dark brown skin. He had his hands properly placed on his desk and sat up straight like a British girl in finishing school.

"Chris man, chill out," his slouching neighbor said.

"How can I chill when we're placed in this life skills class, trying to learn how to deal with our issues from some-one who doesn't know what it's like to be us?"

"Young man," the teacher said, "if you don't like it, you can leave."

Chris stood. His perfectly creased jeans fell over the top of his Timberland boots and I watched each step he took until finally he disappeared into the hallway.

"Anyone else have a problem?" Ms. Finley asked.

"Man, you didn't have to kick him out like that," the neighbor said again.

"Would you like to join him?"

Silence fell over the classroom. Rolling eyes and lip smacks replaced the words I think some wanted to say.

The teacher continued, "We were talking about gender roles. If you open your books to page 107, we will read the chapter aloud..."

She kept talking and I drifted into a daydream. I thought about Jovan and Tisha. It was hard not being able to see them in the hallway and what was I going to do at lunch time? I felt alone. I took out my notebook and started making a list of things I needed to do to get home. Number one...find some money.

"...anyone know what that means?" Ms. Finley interrupted my thoughts. When no one responded, she went into a long spiel about how during Christmas dinner at her house, her father always sat at the head of the table. She followed her story up with some definitions from the book. After a while, I yawned.

Chris was right about this class. Here she is talking about her father sitting at the head of the dinner table, while mine is on the front lines in Iraq. I tuned her out again.

Number two, book a bus ticket, and last but not least, get out of the house without Aunt Sheila knowing.

I looked over my list. Now I had to get to work.

I spent my whole lunch period in the library looking online for buses to Houston. I decided I needed to leave early, while Aunt Sheila was at work, which meant Thursday morning if I planned on being there by Friday. There was only one bus and it left at 11:15 am and got into Houston at midnight. Perfect. Somehow, after Aunt Sheila dropped me at school, I could go back to the house, get my things and head to the bus station. I stored the phone number in my phone and wrote down the address in my notebook. I also set myself a reminder to call and check the availability of seat on the bus.

After looking up fares, I read more news reports on line. I'm sure Tasha and Tisha will not be going to New Orleans. From what I can tell, no one will. Every report I saw, said retuning to New Orleans was not an option at this point. Maybe I can have Tasha drive me to Baton Rouge? I will be sure to ask Tisha tonight.

Next I sent my Daddy an email and told him I needed

money for school clothes. Sure it was a lie, but I'd apologize later. Finally, I checked 411.com for taxi services in Little Rock. There were only a few. I stored the number to the yellow cab company in my phone also. I reviewed my list again. All that's left was to get out of the house without Aunt Sheila knowing. When I thought about it I didn't know her work schedule. In fact, I'm not even for sure what kind of work she does. On top of it all I didn't even have a door key

Maybe I can leave the back door open, I thought.
I made a mental note to scope out the place when I get back. Surely, I can make this work. I logged off of the computer and stared down at my list one last time.

For some reason, I knew number three was going to be the hardest task to scratch off...

Chapter Twenty Two

"Ocean, wait up," I didn't even have to turn around to know it was Gabriella. I hadn't made any other friends the whole day. I had almost made it to the bottom of the hill in front of the school to wait for Aunt Sheila. I didn't want to be rude, so I stopped and faced her.

"What you got up for the rest of the week?" she asked.

Getting the hell up out of here, I thought. "Nothing. Why what's up?" I asked.

"Chris want to get at you?

"Chris? Who is Chris?" I asked.

"He in yo parenting class."

"I'm cool on that," I replied, remembering the well put together guy who had gotten kicked out of class. "I have a man."

"That's what's up then. Yo' man got a friend?" She smiled big, exposing all her teeth.

"I'm sure he has some where he is, but right now, we don't know where any of the old ones are."

I could tell that Gabriella felt bad for asking because her smile faded into a pity frown.

"I'm sorry," she said. "I guess I hadn't thought about what's happening with you."

"It's cool. Like my daddy says, the world don't stop because I'm going through something."

"It must be hard though. Who you living with here?"

"My Aunt Sheila," I said.

"Well at least you have family."

I wish I felt the same way. Maybe I should have been honest and said my alcoholic Aunt Sheila. We sat down on the steps and Gabriella continued to ask questions.

"So did you come before or after the storm?"

"My daddy put me on a bus before the storm hit."

"At least you made it out. From what I see on TV, a lot of people didn't."

I could have just given Gabriella a "yeah, I am lucky reply" but I didn't. For some reason I feel comfortable with her. So I decided to be honest.

"I don't feel lucky," I said, "I wish I was there."

"Girl, you crazy. I would have been out when the first siren went off."

"You say that because y'all don't get hurricanes here. But I've been around them all my life. I think this one caught us off guard."

It took her a second to reply. I guess I had made her think.

"I guess you right," she said. "But we do get tornados and you best believe I am the first one in the tub with a mattress over my head."

I laughed at the way she was demonstrating how she would be hiding in the tub. She looked like she was playing a bad game of charades.

"You laughing. I'm for real," she continued. "I don't play no games when it comes to my life."

I continued to laugh, but it soon came to an end when I saw Aunt Sheila's beat down car coming up the block.

"There's my Aunt," I said.

"Where?"

"Right there," I pointed toward the car.

"Shermed out Sheila yo aunt? Girl that's who you live wit?"

"Unfortunately."

"You right up the block from me. I can't believe you live with her though. Not to talk about your aunt and all, but everybody know she crazy."

I was surprised to find that Gabriella knew Aunt Sheila, but eager to know what she knew.

"What do you mean?" I asked.

"She used to throw these parties at her house all the time. Her and my cousin used to hang real tough. Rumor has it that she got hold of some bad weed."

I think I understand what Gabriella was saying. I had heard of people losing their mind after smoking sherm. In fact, I went to school with a boy in New Orleans who tried it. He ain't been right since.

I always knew Aunt Sheila had a drinking problem, but never knew she smoked marijuana. I guess that explains why she wigs out all the time.

"I won't be there long," I confessed.

"I don't blame you. Sometimes I see your Aunt walking around the 'hood talking to herself."

What she said bothered me. Surely my father didn't know or else he would have never sent me here. If I had any second thoughts about leaving before (which I didn't), they were all out the window now. No way I'm living with a sherm head.

As Gabriella and I said our goodbyes, Aunt Sheila had pulled up in front of the steps. I got in the front seat. I paid close attention to her. She was wearing stretch pants and a fitted tank. Although it wasn't cold, she had on a pair of boots and a jacket. Also, for the first time, I noticed every once in a while it took her eyes a while to focus.

"So how was your first day?" she asked.

"It was cool," I said.

"I see you met a friend."

"Yeah," I said, hoping she would stop with the small talk. I was more afraid of her now.

"You get in your classes okay?"

"Yes ma'am," I said, trying to be a polite as possible. I don't want to make her mad. I just wanted to get through the next two days and get out of here.

I guess being nice worked because she didn't say another word to me until we got to her house. To my surprise, she parked her car and turned off the engine and asked, "You got some money?"

"No ma'am," I replied.

Before she said another word, she let out a loud cackle,

"Me either," she was cracking herself up.

"I'm going to take a walk," I said in a desperate attempt to get away from her.

"Not around here, you won't. This ain't that high falooting stuff you used to with Momma and Willie."

Surely she doesn't think that this place is worse than New Orleans? At any rate, I wasn't messing with her. "You're right," I said. "I'll just go upstairs."

She opened her door. "Good idea," she said.

We both got out of the car and went in the house.

Once I made it inside, I looked around my room. I could never get used to this place. The run down furniture and smell of moth balls was enough to make me miss the newly remodeled house that I only had a chance to live in for a year before Katrina took it away. My daddy worked hard to save for everything he had done. I was proud to finally have a room that I decorated myself.

I sat down on the bed and took out my cell phone. I dialed Jovan and Tisha. Neither of them answered. I then tried my grandma's home number. Another leap of faith, but it was worth the try. After that I did my usual—listened to my iPod until there was something better to do.

❖   ❖   ❖

The "something better" came the next morning.

I couldn't believe I'd fallen asleep and hadn't woken up until Sheila was telling me it was time to get ready for school. I had slept in my clothes, shoes and all. The first thing I did when I realized what time it was was look at my cell phone; I had five missed calls, three from Tisha and two from Jovan. They had both sent me text messages too. I quickly dialed Jovan back.

"Hey," he said when he picked up.

"I was asleep when you called."

"It's all good. I was just checking on you. Are you still trying to come here?"

"Oh yeah. I met a girl at school yesterday who told me that Aunt Sheila is shermed out."

"For real. Your daddy would flip out if he knew that."

"I know, right? So you know I gotta get out of here."

"Why won't you just tell your daddy?"

"He has too much to worry about already. He is trying to come home."

"I know you are happy and I guess you are right."

"I'm happy, but I don't think about it. He says he is still

waiting on paperwork. I don't know how long that will take, so I try not to get excited."

"Well, I chopped it up yesterday with my host family. They said they cool with you coming here as long as we respect they house."

I felt another cloud being lifted from my life. I had a place to go and I will be with Jovan.

"Are you for real?" I asked.

"Yeah. It's an okay little set up."

I guess tragedies bring out the best in people.

"I'm coming," I said, "just got to figure out how. But I will be there by the weekend."

"You got money?"

"Not at all, but I asked my dad for some yesterday."

"I got a little bit. If you need it, I can wire it to you."

"I may need you to do that."

"I'll take care of it today."

"Okay. I'm in Little Rock, AR."

"I know where you at. I wanna see you so bad. I been having dreams about that place."

We shared a laugh. "I miss you too, baby."

"I'll see you this weekend."

"No doubt," I said.

By the time we finished our conversation, I was on cloud nine. I dressed for school and breezed through the day. Of course I saw Gabriella, but even her talking didn't bother me. I was focused on getting to Jovan and away from Sheila. By the time 3:45 came, I had figured out that I would have to walk to the mall up the street when Sheila dropped me off on Thursday and catch a taxi home to get my things. From there I could go pick up the money and go straight to the bus station. There was no stopping me. I had my plan. The only thing left to do is to find out if Tasha could drive me to Baton Rouge (although if she can't, I will find a way). One more day at Hall High, and then I'd be on a one-way ticket back to people that I knew loved me.

Chapter Twenty Three

"Ocean!" Sheila yelled. "Where the hell are my red heels!"

What is she talking about? I don't know anything about her shoes? "What red heels?" I yelled back.

"The ones that tie up my leg!"

"I've never seen them before."

"Well they were in my closet. I'm sure they didn't walk away." She was now standing in my doorway, putting on her earrings.

"Maybe I can help you look for them," I suggested. I didn't want to set her off.

"I don't have time. You got some heels?" she asked, then opened my closet. She reached for my flip flops.

"These will work," she said, then left my room.

Whatever, I thought. I waited awhile until I heard the

front door close then went to the kitchen. I'm glad she left. I hadn't had a chance to look around the house and it was already Wednesday night. I went to the back door; it had a turn lock and a deadbolt. This is going to be easier than I thought. I opened the door and looked outside. It lead into the back yard that looked like it hadn't been cut all summer. I didn't care though. A little grass wouldn't hurt.

When I made it back to my room, I called Greyhound to make sure they had seats available on the bus. After that I phoned Western Union. Jovan had sent two hundred dollars in my name. That would give me enough to pay for the taxi and get my ticket. I packed my things and put them inside the closet. That way I could just grab them in the morning and be gone. After everything was set, I texted Tisha.

See you tomorrow, I wrote.

I can't wait.

Me either.

You won't believe what I'm going through.

Oh no, I thought. I hope I'm not leaving one crazy place just to go to another. *What?*

Well, I guess you were right about Charles.

What happened?

He gave me chlamydia.

What!?! When did you find out?
Monday. Tasha took me to the clinic.

I dialed her number. We could not possibly talk about this over text message.

"What now?" I asked when she answered.

"I can't believe it Ocean. I let him talk me into not using protection."

"Did you tell him?"

"He doesn't answer my calls. At first I thought it was just because of the hurricane, but I was on MySpace yesterday. It said he was logged on, so I sent him a message telling him that we needed to talk. He wrote back and said we had nothing to talk about," she paused for a moment. I could tell she was crying.

"I wrote him back, but he never replied. So when I looked at his page, he had another girl who was his top friend and she had left a comment saying how much she loves him."

I continued to listen. I figured this wasn't the time for me to chastise her about her poor decision making. She continued to tell me that she felt stupid and like her life was over. I assured her it wasn't. I couldn't help but think, though, that she was lucky she only got chlamydia. At least it's curable—it could've been a baby or HIV. Finally I told her we'd talk about it when I got there.

"Okay," she said. "What time does your bus get in?"

"Midnight," I replied. "I've got some stuff to fill you in on too."

"Okay. I can't wait until you get here."

"Me either. And don't worry, we'll be fine."

"I needed to hear that from you Ocean," she said.

Although I still didn't get to ask if Tasha would drive me to Baton Rouge, when we hung up, I felt like my old self again. Before I went to bed for what I hoped was my last night in Little Rock, I thought about a book title I had seen in the book store once and texted it to Tisha:

Boys are stupid, throw rocks at them.

Then I decided she needed some encouragement as well, so I told her what my daddy would say:

Mature people are made, one mistake at a time.

Chapter Twenty Four

I couldn't sleep for thinking about tomorrow.

I lay in the bed staring at the ceiling. The thought of seeing Tisha and Jovan made me feel like a small child on Christmas morning. The only other thing that would've felt better was seeing Daddy and Grandma. After about five minutes, I heard Sheila pull into the driveway. The sound of the engine faded and I could hear her flapping up the steps in my flip flops, then her keys searching for the lock at the front door. After awhile, the door bell rang. I sat up on the edge of the bed placing my feet on the cold hard wood floor.

"I'm coming," I said as I navigated my way toward the front door despite the darkness of the living room.

"Why didn't you leave the damn porch light on?" Sheila demanded before staggering into the open doorway. Oh no, I thought. What do I say? I hadn't even touched the porch light.

"I knew I would be waiting up for you. I just wanted to save some electricity," I lied.

"Do you pay the bill? Got me out here in the dark trying to find the key hole," Aunt Sheila snapped back before falling helplessly into my arms.

Bracing myself for the fall, I tried to help her to her feet without losing my own balance. Sheila smelled of cigarette smoke. And from the looks of things, she must have found her red heels, which where dangling from her left hand like expensive wind chimes.

"Let me go," Sheila demanded, "I ain't drunk. And what you still doing up? Don't you got to go to school tomorrow?"

"Yes ma'am."

"Well go to bed," she waved her hand in the air as if to shoo me away.

I was glad. "Wait," she said right before I made it to my bedroom door, "Come back."

I did as I was told. No sense in making her mad.

Once I got close to her, she said, "Let me tell you something."

She grabbed my face and I was surprised by how warm her touch was. I just expected it to be cold and stiff, like I imagined her heart is.

"Get your education. You don't want to be like me."

She let me go and then crumbled onto the sofa. She landed there spread eagle, exposing her red panties and a tattoo on the inside of her thigh. I leaned in closer to see if I could make out what it was.

I wasn't ready for what I saw.

To my utmost surprise, it said my name, Ocean Renee Sims, with my birthday directly underneath. I had pushed it to the back of my mind because I didn't want it to be true, but was Sheila really my mother? Had what she written in that letter been the truth about my life? I found myself wondering what kind of person she was before she went off the deep end. Had she loved me so much all those years that she kept the secret because she thought it was best for me? Had she been drowning her guilt in alcohol and drugs?

I grabbed the comforter from her bed and covered her, and then leaned in and kissed her cheek. "Goodnight," I said, before walking back to my room. I think I finally understood why I ended up in Little Rock. It had nothing to do with me and everything to do with Sheila.

Chapter Twenty Five

I awoke to the smell of eggs and pancakes. Aunt Shelia had prepared breakfast.

"You up?" She stuck her head in my door.

"Yes ma'am," I replied.

"Well come eat."

I got out of bed and went to the bathroom to get myself together. As I brushed my teeth, I went over my plan carefully in my head, reminding myself to leave the back door unlocked. After washing my face, I joined Aunt Shelia in the kitchen. She was snapping her fingers to Aretha Franklin and pulling the toast out of the oven. I hadn't seen her this happy since I got here.

"So you like school?"

"Yes ma'am," I replied, really I didn't pay enough attention to know if I liked it or not.

I sat down at the table in front of a plate and glass of orange juice she had already prepared. A few seconds later she put a piece of toast on my plate, then sat down across from me. I was afraid to speak while we ate. I didn't want to take the chance of accidentally mentioning my plan to leave. So I forced down the extra dry pancakes and hard eggs without a sound. I watched her as she ate. She was careful not to let any of her food touch; somehow she managed to keep the syrup from everything but her pancakes.

I did not know what to think. I'm not sure why she decided to cook me breakfast, I guess I can call it my last meal in Arkansas. It was a nice gesture, but I'm still leaving.

"Why are your things packed in the closet?" She asked.

My stomach dropped and I looked up at her. Surely she didn't know. As I was trying to think of a story, she spoke again.

"You should make yourself at home. You will probably have to stay here a while. Even when Willie gets back, he won't have a place to go either."

I breathed a sigh of relief. For a minute I thought she had uncovered my plan to leave.

"Yes ma'am," I replied.

Without another word she got up, put her plate in the

sink and disappeared into her bedroom. I was glad; I had eaten more of her breakfast than I could take, plus it was my chance to unlock the back door. I scrapped the rest of the food from my plate into the trash can, then put the plate in the sink. Before I exited the kitchen, I unlocked both the deadbolt and the bottom lock. Afterward, I went to get dressed for school.

It didn't take me long. I knew I had to wear something comfortable for the bus ride, so I put on a pair of jeans and a sweatshirt. A few minutes later Shelia was at my room door.

"You ready?" She asked.

"Yes ma'am," I said. I guess I could fix my hair in the car.

I picked up my back pack from the floor and followed her out of the front door and into the car.

"I don't get of off work until four, so I will be a little late picking you up today," she said.

Perfect. I will be long gone. I looked down at my cell phone; it was almost 8:30. In only four hours I would be on the bus headed back to Houston. The thought of seeing Tisha and Jovan, made me feel good inside. I glanced over at Aunt Shelia. She was dressed in yet another horrible outfit. (I have no idea where she works. But it can't be anywhere nice, if they let her wear that). As I examined her, I thought about last night. For some reason, in that instant, I stopped being angry at her. Maybe it's because I know I won't have to see her after she drops me off, or maybe it's because I believe more today that she is my mother, than I have since she gave me the letter. I know I have to tell her that I'm not mad. I'm not sure why, but something tells me I should. Nevertheless, this is not the place or time.

Finally we pulled up in front of the school.

"Have a good day," she said as I got out of the car.

"You too," I replied and gave her a smile.

I'm not sure what just happened, but whatever it was, for just a second I felt connected to Shelia. I closed the door and walked up the hill. As soon as her car was no longer in sight, I dialed the taxi number from my cell phone and told them to pick me up from the mall in fifteen minutes. Moments later I was walking up "H" street headed to Park Plaza Mall.

When the taxi picked me up, my first stop was Western Union to get Jovan's wire; afterwards the driver took me back to Shelia's to get my things. I went in through the back door, grabbed my suitcase from the closet and put everything that I had not yet packed inside. Before I left I quickly made up the bed. After I was done, I grabbed my suitcase, and then ran back outside to the cab.

I didn't look back.

"Where to now?" The young driver asked. I couldn't help but wonder why he was driving taxi's. He looked young enough to still be in school.

"The Greyhound Bus Station."

He shifted into reverse and backed out of the driveway. As we drove away, I pulled my notebook and pen from my back pack. I started to write my daddy, but I knew that this time was different.

I needed to write my mother, Sheila Renee Sims.

Chapter Twenty Six

Sheila,

By the time you get this, I will be gone. Gone from the pain you have caused me since I came here. I must admit, until last night, I hated you. I hated you for drinking and for not wanting me.

It was not until I saw my named inked into your skin, that I realized that you just might love me. I want you to know that I understand. One thing my father says to me all the time, is that a life without love is an empty life. I never understood what that meant until I witnessed just how empty your life has been. You said in your letter, that you have used alcohol to try to escape the pain of not keeping me.

You don't have to hurt anymore. I have lived a life full of love. Sure, sometimes I wondered what it would have been like to have a mother, but my grandma was so good to me that thought didn't hang around long. I keep the faith that when I get back to New Orleans, she will be there waiting for me, although deep down I know it might not happen.

I once read that true love is not about finding the perfect person, but loving a person perfectly despite their imperfections. Because I'm sure that this is true, I can confidently say that I love you and I hope one day that you will love yourself enough to get help dealing with your addictions. I've realized in only a short time that my life is changed forever. I have no choice but to begin a new one. Take care of yourself.

Love,

Ocean

I closed my notebook.

I felt peaceful. This was the last chapter I needed to write in the book about the first seventeen years of my life. For most, graduation from high school is the rite of passage into change, but Hurricane Katrina opened my door before I had even finished my junior year. Although I've tried so hard to close it, I'm now ready to walk through. My daddy taught me how to love others with compassion. But Katrina has shown me that just in case those people are not around, when it's all said and done I must first *Love...Ocean.*

Letter From the Author

Thank you so much for taking the time to read my novel. Hurricane Katrina taught us all that love is the glue that holds our community together, a lesson that is also true for my life.

Some like to say that I have done some amazing things, but the truth is I have had some amazing support. I have never achieved any task alone. And in this case, things are no different. It is you, the reader, who makes all of this happen for me. Yes, I could have written a line "thanking my fans" in the acknowledgements, but you deserve so much more than that. I want to share a piece of my success with you.

For that reason, I host the Young Minds Writing Contest for young adults (visit my web-site www.celiaanderson.com for more information). The 2008 winner is Terry T-Jay Johnson, graduate of Central High school in Little Rock, AR. I had a lot of great entries; nevertheless, Terry's poem Pink Bread *was written with such raw emotion and grace, that in the end I had to choose him. Although, he claims music as his first love, his writing is equally as enjoyable. It is my pleasure to share his work with the world. Hope you all enjoy. Many Blessings...*

Pink Bread

Mama told me what divorce meant
but I already knew it meant Daddy did dirt
I remembered his two a.m. visits
to a house full of fiends and needles,
with Terrence, only four weeks old, and me in tow.
we would sit on the cold linoleum floor
and wait. Terrence coughed
shirtless in the bitter fall breeze.

I knew that divorce meant
instead of deli meat and mustard,
we had red hot dogs that turned the bread pink.
there was no more Kool-Aid in the house;
Flavor-Aid was all Mama could afford.
Cereal came in Plastic bags, no cardboard boxes
with toys at the bottom.

I stopped asking for birthday parties at seven,
and watched my family while Mama worked
the graveyard shift. I explained to Terrence
that I was the man of the house now.
I took on the responsibility of a man
who left me empty like the syringes that filled
his veins. Mama didn't have to tell me
what divorce meant.

T. Johnson